NEI

It was crude, it w
going about it. F
out between the
to do it than in t
proper boxing match,' Clive said.
Boys' Club, a fortnight from today. Agreed?'

The two combatants shuffled their feet and avoided looking at each other. 'All right,' Mike Young said finally.

Clive turned to the other young warrior. 'Shane?'

'Ah . . . he'll keep till then, I guess,' Shane Ramsay muttered. 'That's if he keeps away from Jane.'

Ah yes, the young lady in question, the immediate cause of the hostilities – Jane Harris, the pretty temptress who could provoke such passions in Ramsay Street. 'Let them fight,' she cried angrily to Clive Gibbons who had just stepped in to pull the fighting pair apart and thus create a very fragile peace in the street for the time being. 'Let them kill each other for all I care,' she said, striding away and leaving the three of them to stare after her with their mouths open.

Also by Carl Ruhen in Star Books

NEIGHBOURS 1
NEIGHBOURS 2
NEIGHBOURS 3
NEIGHBOURS 4
NEIGHBOURS 5
NEIGHBOURS 6

NEIGHBOURS™ 7

Carl Ruhen

From an original concept by Bill Searle, Rick Maier, Dave Worthington, John Linton, Ginny Loundes, Ray Harding, Ysabelle Dean, Ray Kolle, John Upton, Lois Booton, Betty Quin, Penny Fraser, David Phillips, Reg Watson, Greg Millin, Christine McCourt, Jeffrey Truman, Tarquin Scott, Cheredith Mok, Wayne Doyle

A STAR BOOK
Published by
the Paperback Division of
W. H. Allen & Co Plc

A Star Book
Published in 1989
by the Paperback Division of
W. H. Allen & Co Plc
Sekforde House, 175–9 St John Street,
London, EC1V 4LL

Printed and bound in Great Britain by
Anchor Press Ltd, Tiptree, Essex

ISBN 0 352 32384 1

One

The trouble was, Charlene just couldn't remember what did happen at that party. She tried hard to remember, she really wracked her brains over it, but it was impossible. All she could manage to summon up were faint, blurred images, as well as an overriding impression of relentless noise, that were disconnected and meaningless. And it was important – no, vital – that she remember; they were on her back about it, demanding to know what the hell had happened at that party that had led to Warren Murphy being bashed so viciously that he was now lying unconscious in hospital with all sorts of tubes sticking out of him.

'You were there.' Ray Murphy was glaring at her with narrowed, angry eyes. 'You *must* know what happened.'

But Charlene didn't. She hadn't the vaguest idea of what had happened except that she'd had too much to drink. 'I don't know . . .' She shook her head unhappily. 'Nothing.'

'Don't give me that,' Ray Murphy snapped. 'You were with him.'

Charlene, in a state of fuzziness, her head still throbbing even after the aspirin and strong black coffee, was copping it from all sides this morning; her cousin Shane had been laying down the law just because Charlene's mother had made him responsible for her while she was away. It was about time she obeyed a few house rules, he had told her, and instead of late and boozy nights with Warren Murphy, who drank too much for his own good anyway, there were her coming school examinations to think about. Charlene had been listening to him with gloom and a throbbing head when Ray Murphy had turned up with the news that his son had been found by the police in the gutter near his home and taken to hospital. Charlene was shocked. Shane was shocked. Ray Murphy was furious.

'Well?' he demanded. 'Did he get into a fight?'

'I don't know.' Charlene shrugged helplessly.

'Look, Charlene . . .' Shane advanced on her; Charlene backed away.

'We got to the party,' she said weakly. 'He introduced me to a couple of his friends, and then . . .'

'Then what?' Ray Murphy prompted.

She was trying very hard, but it was no use. 'I don't remember,' she said at last. She felt awful.

There had been two parties in fact. The first one, at Gerry Butler's was no problem. She could remember what had happened there, more or less, although they'd had quite an amount to drink by the time they left. Mostly it had been kids from school, letting their hair down in a last chance to have some fun before the examinations. Charlene had exchanged a few sharp words with the nasty-minded Sue Parker, who had made play of the fact that Charlene had come to the party with Warren rather than Scott Robinson which was what everyone would have expected, unless of course he had come to his senses and taken up with someone else. Charlene hadn't bothered to explain that Scott had decided to remain at home to do some studying even if it *was* Saturday night and there was a party at Gerry Butler's place. Then, at around midnight, the drink had run out, and Warren had suggested to Charlene that they check out another party he knew about, over at Waratah Street – some friends of his who would have plenty of booze for sure. Charlene had been hesitant, but he had managed to persuade her. And it was at about this point that her memory began to fail her.

'Anyway, the police will want to have a word with you,' Ray Murphy said. 'They're at the hospital now.'

'Me?' Charlene asked in a nervous voice. 'Why me?'

'You were with him, weren't you?'

'Yes, but I told you . . . I don't remember.' She appealed to Shane. 'Do I have to?'

'It's all right,' Shane reassured her. 'I'll be with you.'

'What do I say to them?'

'The truth,' Ray Murphy said shortly as he moved across to the kitchen door. 'Now come on, we're wasting time.'

Charlene hesitated; Shane took her arm. 'The police only want to help,' he said gently. 'If they get too tough, well, I'll sort it out.' He gave her a brave smile, then led her to the door which Ray Murphy was holding open for them with a frown of impatience.

At the hospital, after she had been taken to one side by the two waiting policemen, there were more questions. 'Did you know any of the other kids at the second party?' she was asked.

'Not really.' Charlene was still thinking hard; she was very nervous. 'They were mostly Warren's friends. I had seen a few of them around before, but that's all.'

One of the policemen asked the questions while the

other took notes. Further along the hospital corridor Shane and Ray Murphy were waiting outside the door of Warren's room. 'Were there any that showed a dislike for him?'

'No.' Charlene was quite certain of that much at least. 'Everyone seemed to get along.'

'Are you sure about that?'

'Yeah . . .' As far as she could remember, anyway.

'When did you leave the party?'

'Early morning.' It was the best she could do. The second policeman made a note in his book.

'With Warren Murphy?'

'I guess so.'

'You don't know?' The questioner regarded her steadily. Charlene, conscious of the trembling of her lower lip, looked away from him.

'I suppose I did.'

'Why aren't you sure?'

A trolley pushed by an orderly in a white coat rattled past them. 'I had a bit to drink,' Charlene murmured guiltily.

'Then what *do* you remember?'

Charlene was becoming quite desperate; it was all such a maddening haze. 'We arrived there together,' she said slowly. 'I mean, he brought me there from the first party. We were drinking, and I had a dance with some guy.' She shook her head. 'That's all I can remember. Honest.'

'Just the one guy, was it?'

'Yeah. I'm sure.'

'Was Warren jealous when you did that?'

'Why should he be?' Some of Charlene's old spirit was returning. 'He's not my boyfriend, or anything like that. And, anyway, I've told you all I know about it. Why don't you ask some of the other kids who were at that party?'

'We intend to do just that, Miss Mitchell,' the policeman said with a nod to his partner, who closed his notebook and put away his pen. 'But if you *do* remember anything more, we'd like to hear about it.'

'Okay.'

After stopping briefly to exchange a few words with Ray Murphy, they moved off down the corridor. Charlene joined Shane and Murphy outside Warren's room. As she sat down beside them, Murphy gave her a sour look which made her feel even worse, if that was possible. As if she had been directly responsible in some way for his son being beaten up – part of the conspiracy, leading him into the trap, pointing the finger and saying, 'There he is, boys, get stuck into him.' It was stupid, ridiculous. It was very unfair to be blaming her like this. The door opposite them opened and a crisp-looking woman doctor stepped out into the corridor. She looked inquiringly at Ray.

'Mister Murphy?'

Ray Murphy was on his feet, his leathery face creased in concern. 'How is he? Is he going to be okay?'

'Your son briefly regained consciousness,' she told him.

'So?' Ray was showing his anxiety. 'Well, for God's sake, tell me. Is he going to be all right?'

'It could have been much worse,' she said. 'He was lucky. His left arm is broken, and there is extensive bruising and lacerations. There's also a swelling on the back of his head.' She shrugged briefly. 'We'll know more when the results of the tests are through.'

'Did he say anything?' Ray demanded.

The doctor turned to Charlene. 'Are you Charlene?' Charlene nodded. 'He wanted to know if Charlene was all right,' the doctor told Ray. 'He seemed quite worried about her.'

Murphy rounded on Charlene. 'If you know anything, you'd better start talking,' he said in a threatening tone.

Charlene was close to tears. 'I wish I did . . .'

Shane stepped forward. 'Lay off, Ray,' he said firmly. 'She would have told the police if she knew anything.' He turned to Charlene. 'Come on, I'll take you home.'

The doctor had gone back into the room. Ray had slumped back onto the seat. Charlene stared pleadingly down at him. 'It wasn't my fault. You've got to believe me.' Ray continued to sit despondently, rebuking her with his silence. Charlene kept trying. 'Warren's got his faults, I know. He didn't get along with every kid at school. I mean, no one would ever say that he was popular. But that doesn't mean . . . Look, I wouldn't do anything to see him hurt.'

Ray looked blankly up at her. 'Seventeen years of age,' he murmured distractedly. 'He's just a pup.'

Charlene sat down beside him. 'I reckon I'd like to be left alone,' Ray muttered.

Rising again to her feet, Charlene began to back away from him with the awful realisation that there was no way she could get through to him, make him see that she was telling the truth, that she really *didn't* know what happened at the party last night. If only she hadn't had so much to drink. She cursed herself for not having remained sober enough to remember what did happen. She was such a fool.

Leaving Ray Murphy to continue his sad vigil outside his son's room, Shane and Charlene returned to Ramsay Street by taxi. Scott Robinson was waiting for them outside the Ramsay house. Oh God, Charlene thought woefully when she saw him, this is all I need now.

She tried to avoid him, but he caught up with her. 'Charlene, I've got some questions to ask you.'

Questions, questions – everyone had questions to ask her; they were loading her with questions she couldn't answer. 'Get off, will you!' she snapped, pushing past him.

He grabbed her arm. 'We've got to talk,' he said urgently. 'About what happened. With Warren.'

So the news had already got out. 'Can't it wait?'

'I want to know what happened between you and Warren.'

'Give it a break, will you.' Charlene could feel herself losing control. 'I feel bad enough as it is.'

'Yes, I'll bet.' His fingers were digging into her arm.

'Let her go, Scott,' Shane said, coming up to them. 'Just give her a bit of time. It's been a rough morning for all of us.'

It was at this point that Mrs Mangel, who had been observing them all from her front lawn, decided to offer her own contribution to the scene that was being enacted in what had, until a few minutes earlier, been the Sunday morning calm of Ramsay Street. 'Do you three mind keeping your arguments to yourselves?' she called. 'You're disturbing the whole street with your carry on – and it *is* Sunday morning.'

Angrily, Charlene pulled herself free from Scott's grasp. 'I don't hear anyone else complaining,' she yelled. 'You old cow,' she added for good measure.

Mrs Mangel gasped. Her long nose quivered. 'Such insolence!' she said in a voice of outrage, her finger pointed accusingly at Charlene. 'I've had just about enough of you, young lady. You should be taken down a peg or two, the way you're behaving.'

'Don't worry, Mrs Mangel.' Shane was trying to keep the peace. 'I'll look after her.'

Mrs Mangel was a picture of affronted dignity. 'In *my* day,' she sniffed, 'you would have received a good hiding for talking to your elders like that.'

'Stupid cow,' Charlene muttered as Mrs Mangel moved stiffly back into her house, slamming the front door behind her.

'But she's right, though,' Scott said tightly. 'It *is* about time you were taught a lesson.'

Charlene stared at him in surprise. Did she hear him right? Was he actually taking Mrs Mangel's side in this? No one took Mrs Mangel's side in anything. She was a . . . a dinosaur; she was extinct but didn't realise it. 'What's got into you?'

'I mean it,' Scott said in disgust. 'I'm sick and tired of the way you use people, especially me.' He turned away from her. 'The next time you find yourself in trouble, don't expect me to pick up the pieces.'

Dismayed, Charlene stared after him as he began to walk away from her. What was bugging him now? Just because she had gone to the party with Warren? She *had* asked him if he wanted to come but he had begged off, saying that he had to study. So . . ? 'Scott,' she called after him as he headed towards his own house, but he didn't stop or give any other sign that he had heard her.

She wanted to be alone. She locked herself in her room and brooded. She felt sorry for herself; she cried a little; she worried about Scott, and about Warren Murphy; she tried to remember what happened at the party; she felt utterly miserable. There was a knock on the door.

'Charlene, do you want anything to eat?' Charlene didn't reply; she wasn't hungry. 'Come on, Charlene, you can't spend the whole day in your room.' Charlene still said nothing; all she wanted was to be left alone.

'Okay, have it your own way.' Shane was obviously becoming exasperated. 'I'm going out.'

A few moments later, Charlene heard the front door closing firmly. She stirred herself from the bed, unlocked the door and stepped hesitantly out into the hallway. She started when she saw Shane standing by the front door. 'I thought you'd gone,' she said reproachfully.

Shane smiled faintly. 'I didn't think you would come out if I was still here.'

Charlene was annoyed with herself for having fallen for the trick. 'I just want to be left alone,' she said, moving towards the front door. 'All right?'

Shane was blocking her way. He shook his head. 'No, you don't.' He gestured towards the kitchen. 'Come on. Come through here and sit down.'

Too exhausted to resist, Charlene allowed herself to be led into the kitchen. 'Do you want something to eat?' Shane asked her. She shook her head as Shane filled the kettle. 'A cup of tea might help.'

'It won't bring Scott back,' Charlene said unhappily. Shane moved across the room to her. 'If Warren hadn't talked me into going to that stupid party, I wouldn't be in this mess.'

Shane regarded her intently. 'Is feeling sorry for yourself going to help?' Charlene didn't reply. No, she didn't see how it would help. 'You didn't have to go,' Shane reminded her. 'And when you did go, you didn't have to drink so much.' He frowned at her. 'Look, Charlene, I've warned you about drinking. Didn't *any* of it sink in?'

'Shane . . .'

'Then why do it?'

'It was a party,' Charlene returned defensively. 'The others were drinking. What else was I supposed to do?'

'You could have said no.'

Oh, what was the use? 'I don't *need* this,' Charlene moaned.

'Oh, yes you do.' Shane followed her into the living room. 'Come on. You're copping out. Just because someone else does something doesn't mean *you* have to do it as well. Does it, Charlene? I mean, you wouldn't go in for shoplifting, for example, just because everyone else is doing it.'

'Of course not.'

'Then you have to stand up for what you want,' Shane said. 'Be different. You never know – you might just be respected for it.'

'And what if I don't respect myself?' There was a long and jarring silence. Charlene felt herself beginning to panic. 'I don't even know how long I was at that second party. Or if I saw Warren being bashed.' There were tears in her eyes, a catch in her voice. 'I don't remember anything.'

Shane took her in his arms as she began to cry, and tried to comfort her. 'Come on, it's all right,' he said soothingly. 'We all make mistakes. You just have to learn not to make the same one again.'

Charlene clung to him. She needed him and every scrap of emotional support he could offer her.

She was feeling a little better that afternoon as she sat at the dining room table surrounded by her school text books and prepared herself for some solid study. However onerous it might be for her, at least it helped take her mind off her other problems. But she hard hardly settled down to it when those problems were thrust back at her with the arrival of Ray Murphy, whose attitude was more than a little aggressive.

'Now, look,' he said after he had pushed past Shane to confront Charlene, 'I'm not a man who is used to doing things twice. And I'm not a man who stands by while some people laugh behind my back.'

Charlene looked blankly up at him. Now what? 'I don't . . .'

'I've talked to some of the kids who were at that party last night,' he said.

Shane had come into the room behind him. 'Relax, Ray,' he said. 'She has already explained . . .'

But Ray Murphy wasn't listenng to him; he didn't take his eyes off Charlene. 'And they tell me that you were with Warren all night.' He gestured angrily. 'All flamin' night.'

'Mister Murphy . . .'

'So one wouldn't have to be exactly brilliant to figure out that you know exactly what happened to him.' His eyes were hard; the skin was stretched tautly over his high cheekbones. 'Do you know what I think?'

Charlene was still trying to protest. 'Mister . . .'

'I think you've been feeding me a load of garbage.' He was almost shouting now. 'You're covering up for the mongrels who did this thing to Warren.'

Charlene was horrified by the accusation. 'No!' she exclaimed.

He was leaning over her, his face thrust close to hers. A vein throbbed at his temple. His voice was cutting into her like a knife. 'And don't you lie to me. Don't make it any worse. Warren is lying there, in that hospital, with tubes and God knows what else sticking out of him. They've got him stretched out like a slab of meat, and I want to know who has done it to him.' His flushed face was contorted with rage. Charlene cringed away from him. 'And you're going to tell me, you little . . .'

'That's enough, mate,' Shane said sharply, placing his hand on Murphy's arm.

'That's what you think.' Murphy pushed him away then glowered once more at Charlene. 'You know who they are. You know where they live.'

'That's not true,' Charlene protested feebly.

Shane grabbed Ray Murphy's arm again, this time more forcefully, and swung him away from the table. 'Look, I said that's enough.'

Ray Murphy struggled free then, as Charlene cried out in alarm, aimed a punch at Shane. Shane blocked it with his arm. Catching his balance, Ray prepared to deliver another blow. 'No!' Charlene yelled. 'No! Stop it!'

Ray Murphy was not quick enough. As he brought back his fist again, Shane sprang forward and, catching his arm by the wrist, forced it down and with a quick swivelling motion wrenched it up behind his back. Ray yelped in sudden pain. 'Stop it!' Charlene cried again.

'That's enough, mate.' Shane was still holding Ray's arm up behind his back. 'Fighting is not going to solve anything.'

Ray Murphy was breathing heavily. 'My son's in hospital,' he gasped. 'And I want to know the names of the blokes who put him there.'

Charlene was terrified by what was happening. 'If I knew, I'd tell you!' she screamed.

Sweat was beading Ray's high and narrow forehead as he struggled to free himself from the tight hold Shane had on him. 'Oh . . . you know all right,' he panted.

'Look, this is not going to help Warren, is it?' Shane pointed out. 'She says she doesn't know, and I believe her.'

The telephone began to ring. Ray stopped struggling. 'All right,' he muttered.

'Get that, will you,' Shane said to Charlene, jerking his head to the direction of the telephone.

The call was for Ray Murphy. It was the hospital. 'I left the number here in case there was any change,' he explained as Shane released him. He snatched the receiver out of Charlene's hand. Charlene moved back across the room to stand by Shane's side. 'Thanks,' she heard Ray Murphy say to the caller. 'I'll be straight over.' He replaced the receiver. 'Warren has regained consciousness,' he told Shane. 'I'm going to the hospital.'

'I'll come with you,' Charlene said.

Ray glared at her. 'Like hell you will,' he growled, then turning on his heel, headed quickly for the door.

'At least he's conscious,' Shane remarked after the door had closed behind Murphy. 'Now they can find out what happened.'

Charlene was shaking; she had been quite unnerved by what had happened. 'I should be there.'

'You heard what Ray said.'

'Yes, but . . .'

'You'd better keep out of his way.'

'I don't care.'

'Well, I do,' Shane said. 'If he was mad enough to have a go at me just now, imagine what he'll do to you if you show up at the hospital.'

'I still don't care. I'm going.'

'No, you're not.'

He caught up with her as she moved out into the hallway. 'Come back here,' he ordered, taking hold of her arm. 'You can just think about someone else besides yourself for once. Ray doesn't want you hassling Warren.'

'I don't want to hassle him.'

'Good.' Shane nodded. 'Then you can leave them both alone.'

The back door opened. 'Hello,' Nikki Dennison called as she came into the kitchen.

Shane released Charlene's arm. 'G'day,' he greeted the newcomer. Charlene lapsed into a sulky silence. Here was someone else who was likely to have a go at her.

'Oh, hi Shane. Can I talk to Charlene?'

'Sure.' Shane turned back to his cousin. 'I'm going for a ride on my bike,' he informed her. 'I just hope you won't get any smart ideas about visiting Warren.' Charlene glared at him for a moment then shook her head. It seemed she didn't have much choice in the matter. 'Good.' Shane nodded. 'Keep an eye on her, will you,' he said to Nikki. 'She's been in enough trouble for one day.'

'I suppose you've got a few things to say as well,' Charlene said resentfully after Shane had gone.

They had moved into the living room. 'I just came to see if you were all right,' Nikki said.

Charlene immediately regretted her tone; she was quite touched that Nikki had come to see her. A friendly face, a shoulder to lean on – it was just what she needed. 'Sorry for snapping,' she said, dropping wearily onto the couch. Nikki sat down beside her. 'Oh hell, it's just that everything's such a mess.'

'How's Warren?'

'The hospital called to say that he had regained consciousness, but that's all I know.'

'Well, who beat him up?' Nikki queried.

'I wish I knew.' Charlene sighed heavily and shook her head. 'How could I just black out two hours of my whole life?' Nikki stared at her uncomprehendingly. 'I must have been pretty well out of it,' Charlene elaborated. 'I don't remember anything. Only no one will believe me.' She thought of something. 'Hey, is Scott still mad with me?' she asked.

Nikki was staying with the Robinsons. 'Nothing will convince him that you don't fancy Warren,' she said.

'He's as bad as Shane.' Charlene grimaced. 'Well, I *don't* fancy him – okay?'

'But you just said that you can't remember what happened for two hours,' Nikki gently reminded her. 'How do you know what you and Warren did?'

Charlene didn't know. God, this was getting worse and worse the more she thought about it. 'Oh, this is ridiculous. I don't like Warren in that way. Not like that. You know what I mean.'

'Maybe that's why you can't remember,' Nikki said. 'You've blanked it out on purpose. Maybe you were so drunk that you and Warren . . .'

Charlene didn't let her finish. She flared up at this schoolgirl psychologist who thought she knew all the answers. 'No, Nikki. I don't need that. I *know* I didn't do anything.'

'I hope you're right,' Nikki said rather self-righteously.

Charlene was on guard again. 'What does that mean?'

'It means that Scott is already thinking the worst, and . . . Sue Parker is going to have a field day when she hears about this.'

To hell with Sue Parker. Honestly, the girl was a menace; she'd had her eye on Scott for quite some time now. 'Only if my so-called friends blab about it to her,' Charlene said waspishly.

'I was only trying to help.'

Charlene was no longer touched by Nikki's visit. She had thought Nikki would provide a shoulder for her to lean on, but obviously she had been wrong. Nikki Dennison was no better than any of the others. 'Thanks, but no thanks,' she said bitterly. 'I've had all the sermons I can take.' She turned away. 'I'd rather be left alone.'

'That's fine with me.'

Obviously hurt by Charlene's attitude, Nikki stood up and walked huffily out of the room. As the door closed behind her, Charlene, suddenly realising that she was friendless again, ran after her. 'Nikki,' she called. 'I didn't mean . . .'

But it was no use; Nikki had gone. Alone and dejected, Charlene turned back into the room.

She couldn't stay in the house alone. She was depressed and restless. She decided to get down to the hospital to see how Warren was. She was quite prepared to face his father's hostility once more.

'What are you doing here?' he demanded as she approached him along the hospital corridor.

'Is Warren all right?'

He wasn't pleased to see her. 'We don't know yet,' he said gruffly. 'He was unconscious again when I arrived.'

They were standing outside Warren's room. 'I'd like to see him,' Charlene said nervously.

Ray shook his head grimly. 'I don't want him to have anything to do with you.'

'I've told you I'm sorry.'

Ray regarded her dubiously. 'Yeah, sure.'

'No, honestly,' Charlene insisted. 'I don't remember because I . . . I had too much to drink.'

'You shouldn't be drinking at all if you can't handle it.'

Charlene was stung by his words. 'Then why don't you tell that to your son?' she retorted.

'Don't give me any of your lip,' Ray growled threateningly.

The door opened and a nurse stepped out into the corridor. 'Mister Murphy,' she said, 'your son has just regained consciousness again. You can see him for a few minutes.'

'Thanks.' Ray rose quickly to his feet. Charlene followed him as he headed for the door the nurse was holding open. 'Where do you think *you're* going?' he demanded, rounding on her.

'I don't want to upset him or anything. Please . . .'

'Please keep the noise down,' the nurse admonished them. 'Warren mustn't be upset.'

Charlene was still staring at Ray. 'Please . . .'

Ray regarded her stonily for a long moment, then relented. 'All right,' he said. 'Two minutes, and that's it.'

She hovered by the door as Ray Murphy crossed the room to the bed where his son was lying, his head bandaged and his left arm in a sling. His face was badly bruised and there was a cut on his lower lip.

'G'day, Dad,' he said with a weak smile.

'Oh, mate.' Leaning over the bed, Ray Murphy gave Warren a hug. 'I'm so pleased to see you're all right,' he said with emotion.

'Hey, Dad. Hey, hey, careful of the ribs.'

'Sorry.' Ray straightened. He smiled tremulously. His eyes were glistening. 'I must be getting soft in my old age.'

'I'm okay. Really.'

'Yeah, well . . .' Ray gestured awkwardly, then remembered Charlene in the doorway behind him. 'There's someone else here to see you.'

Charlene came into the room. She tried to smile brightly but was aware of the tremor of her lips. 'Hi,' she said. 'You look like you were hit by a truck.'

'I *feel* like I was hit by a truck,' Warren told her ruefully.

'Yeah, I bet . . .'

He was looking up at her closely. 'Have you told Dad what happened?' he asked.

Charlene looked at Ray who shook his head. 'No, she hasn't,' he said.

'I don't remember,' Charlene said uncomfortably.

Warren grinned. 'Yeah. I guess we were both pretty far gone.'

'That's nothing to be proud of, son,' Ray Murphy said reproachfully.

Warren was still looking up at Charlene. 'Don't you remember going to the party in Waratah Street?'

'Well, yeah . . . but not much after we got there.'

'Not those guys?'

'What guys?' Charlene couldn't remember any guys. She had danced with someone – that was about all she could remember. All the rest was still a haze.

'They were trying to chat you up,' Warren told her. 'I thought I'd better get you home.'

'I don't remember any of that.'

'Yes, well . . . but you can't really blame them,' Warren said. 'I mean, you weren't exactly driving them off.'

Charlene said nothing; she was too embarrassed to speak; she could feel the sudden warmth in her cheeks. 'I see,' Ray Murphy said flatly. 'That's how it was then, was it?'

Seeing that he was becoming angry with her again, Charlene began to protest. 'It's not normally like that . . .'

'Anyway, I got you home,' Warren continued. 'But they must have followed us. Ah. . . .they started hassling me down at the end of Ramsay Street. Then they got heavy and started putting the boot in . . .'

Ray swore softly but explosively. 'Pack of mongrels.' He swung to face Charlene. 'Who were they?' he demanded.

Charlene shook her head. 'I would have told him if I could remember,' she explained to Warren.

But Ray still wasn't convinced. 'She's covering up for them.'

'I'm *not*,' Charlene cried bitterly.

'You . . .'

'Look, it's okay,' Warren broke in hurriedly. 'I've told the police. They've probably already got them by now.'

'Good.' Ray nodded grimly. 'Now you tell me and I'll straighten them out myself.'

'No, Dad.' Warren shook his head. 'There's been enough trouble already. Okay? Just leave it to the cops.'

Ray's thin lips were curved in contempt as he stared at Charlene. 'And who's going to give *her* what she deserves?'

'Dad, it wasn't her fault.'

'But she was encouraging them. You said so yourself.'

'She didn't know what she was doing.'

Charlene was close to tears again. 'Warren, I'm sorry. I really am.'

Ray Murphy snorted in disgust. 'And a fat lot of good that'll do.'

Charlene tried hard to defend herself. 'I didn't know anything like this was going to happen.' How *could* she possibly know?

'Oh, get out!' Ray gestured angrily. 'You make me sick.'

'Don't take it out on her, Dad,' Warren pleaded, as Charlene moved dejectedly to the door.

'She's got off pretty lightly to my way of thinking,' Ray said tautly.

As she came down the front steps of the hospital,

blinking back the tears, Shane pulled up beside her on his motorbike. 'Are you all right?'

'How did you know I was here?'

'You weren't home. I put two and two together. A lucky guess, I suppose.' His expression clouded. 'Look, I told you not to come here. You know the mood Ray is in . . .'

The sun was shining. The car park was full. Sunday visitors drifted towards the hospital entrance with bunches of flowers and bored-looking children. 'I had to see Warren . . . tell him I was sorry.'

Shane made a sound of exasperation. 'What are we going to do with you? Lock you in your room like a little kid?'

'Oh, lay off, Shane!' Charlene snapped. 'Ray has just finished ripping into me.'

'Maybe he should have belted *you* instead of trying it out on me,' Shane said testily. 'It might have knocked some sense into you.' He patted the pillion behind him with his gauntleted hand. 'Come on. Get on.'

'No, thanks.' Charlene shook her head. 'I want to walk home.'

'Charlene . . .'

'I need to think.'

There was a lot to think about; she needed to get matters into some sort of perspective. She was very tired. She began to walk.

Two

Of all the electrical appliances in Erinsborough – that glittering panoply of devices and labour-savers, the battalions of vacuum cleaners and floor polishers, the hordes of television sets and triple-deck stereos, the legions of toasters and microwave ovens, the washing machines, the drying machines, the freezers, the home computers, the tea-making alarm radios, the hair-dryers and portable telephones – of all this fine array of gadgets, the one that was undoubtedly causing the most worry at the moment was the cappuccino machine in Daphne Clarke's coffee shop. Right now it was spurting steam and hissing at her in a most sinister fashion.

'It's going crazy,' Daphne complained as she backed nervously away from it.

The machine rumbled; it released some more steam. All the customers were looking at it with worried expressions. 'I think it's going to blow up,' Daphne said apprehensively.

With one pacifying hand extended, Clive Gibbons advanced cautiously on the delinquent machine. 'Don't worry,' he said. 'It's just being a bit temperamental. It must be one of its off days.' He began to stroke the polished flank of the machine that had been imported from Italy a long time ago, and made soothing noises. 'There, there now . . .' He opened a valve slightly to allow more steam to escape. 'I don't think it's a physical problem,' he pronounced. 'Just overwork. Stress maybe.' He spoke confidentially to the machine; he was employing his best bedside manner. 'Now, look, I know you sometimes get a bit hot under the collar, and you've got more right than most to let off some steam every now and again. But there's no need to blow a gasket.'

Despite her nervousness, Daphne found herself smiling. 'Do you think you could give it a quick tranquillising injection while it's not looking?' she asked.

Clive gave her a stern look. 'What kind of doctor do you think I am?' he demanded. He patted the side of the machine. 'Can you blame this little lady for thinking there's more to life than a constant stream of cappuccinos?'

Daphne pulled a face. 'That's all I need,' she groaned. 'A neurotic cappuccino machine. And a comedian. Anyway, how do you know it's female?'

'I'm a doctor, Daphne,' Clive replied with an expression of reproach. 'Do you really think I can't tell the difference?' He was still gently stroking the machine which was gradually quietening down. 'You see? It's settling down now. A few compassionate words and a gentle hand make all the difference.'

'Now they've made all the difference,' Daphne said drily, 'will it make a cappuccino?'

'I think she's in need of a rest,' Clive replied with a solemn shake of his head.

'Well, I've got an order for one.'

Clive lowered his voice. 'Daphne, the welfare of the patient is my first concern,' he said.

'Thanks a lot, Clive.'

Clive held up his hands. 'I can take no credit for the healing power in these hands,' he said. 'It's a gift. One I share freely with all mankind.'

'Freely?' Daphne raised her eyebrows.

'Well. For the standard fee.'

The machine gave another threatening rumble. 'Clive, I'm calling a service man.'

'Oh, I see.' Clive sounded hurt. 'Referral to a specialist, huh? No faith in your humble GP.'

'This GP isn't so much humble as out of his mind,' Daphne remarked acidly.

The machine hissed loudly and venomously. 'Whoa, whoa,' Clive cried in alarm. 'It looks as though she's the protective type. She is wounded by your hurtful remarks.' Moving across to Daphne, he began to stroke her arm. 'Friend, friend,' he said soothingly to the machine. 'She's a friend.'

Beaming warmly at the customers, Clive pointed to the machine. 'It's all right,' he said reassuringly. 'Just a breakdown. Nervous breakdown.' He continued to stroke Daphne's arm. 'Friend,' he said once more to the machine, giving it a look of anguished sympathy. 'She's a friend.'

The machine continued to be temperamental. 'Clive thinks it may need major surgery,' Daphne told Charlene Mitchell, when she came into the shop later that afternoon.

'Give me a go.' With an air of self-confidence, Charlene moved around behind the counter.

'Careful, Charlene. It bites.'

Charlene picked up a jug of milk and held it against the machine's steam pipe. The rumbling and the hissing stopped. 'Reckon I've got the lucky touch today,' Charlene said with a smirk. 'Maybe I should buy a lottery ticket.'

'I can think of a better way of earning a few dollars,'

Daphne said gratefully. 'Come and work the machine for me.'

Charlene came round from behind the counter. 'Thanks, but I've got to catch up on some studying. Exams, you know.'

'Well, maybe I'll call you if Clive decides that the machine needs some intensive care nursing.'

Charlene grinned at her. 'You will have to wait until I starch my uniform,' she said.

The situation was becoming impossible. What made it worse was that people kept asking for cappuccinos. The machine hissed and bubbled, and refused to co-operate. There was nothing else for it but to call somebody to come and have a look at it.

'Oh, I see someone's in a good mood,' Madge Mitchell said, entering the shop just as Daphne slammed down the telephone receiver.

'Well, it certainly isn't me,' Daphne said sourly. 'They said they would send a repair man . . . four hours ago.'

'Why? Has something broken down?'

Daphne nodded at the machine with its taps and shining surfaces. 'It's this useless thing,' she said in disgust. 'It should be dismantled and used as a pop-up toaster. Nobody seems to know what's wrong with it.' She took a deep breath. Her expression softened. 'Oh, I'm sorry. Can I help you?'

'I'd like a cappuccino,' Madge said, and Daphne threw her hands up in despair.

Clive Gibbons was someone else who wanted coffee. 'What an oasis after the desert I've travelled today,' he cried gratefully as he walked into the shop. He clutched his throat. 'Coffee. I must have coffee. I'm parched.'

'One hump or two?' Daphne asked drily.

Clive grimaced at her. '*I* do the jokes – okay?'

'You do the jokes.'

'So . . .'

'There's no coffee. Your girl-friend has gone on strike again.'

'Prima donna.' Clive touched the machine. 'From Milan. Nicely handled . . .'

'Ah.'

'Nicely handled . . .' Clive drew his hand away. 'She's running quite a temperature.'

'Clive,' Daphne said in exasperation, 'never mind the diagnosis. How do we fix it?'

'Sorry.' Clive glumly shook his head. 'I'm just a GP. Freud works the other side of the street.'

'Clive!'

'All right.' Clive gave a resigned shrug. 'I'll check her out. But you should know that psychoanalysis costs big bikkies, and . . . ah . . . hey.' He started as the machine let off a powerful blast of steam.

Clive consulted with the machine. He coaxed and cajoled, he tinkered and adjusted. 'There you go,' he said finally with a cheesy sort of grin. 'All finished.'

Daphne looked at him in surprise. 'You fixed it?'

Clive nodded in a self-satisfied way. 'Another triumph for medical science.'

'What was the problem?'

'It's what we in the medical profession term a loose screw.'

Daphne was disappointed. 'Clive, why can't you be serious – just for once?'

'I *am* being serious.' He held up the screwdriver with which he had been working on the machine. 'A few turns with my trusty scalpel and *voila*, ze machine, she is fixed.' He fished a slip of paper from his shirt pocket. 'And here is the account,' he said, handing it to her.

Daphne looked at the slip and gasped. 'Twenty-five bucks?'

'Yeah . . . well . . .' Clive reached for his jacket; suddenly he was in a hurry. 'Ah, a few house calls to make.'

Then he was gone. Daphne clenched her fists. 'I'll kill him,' she muttered. 'Honestly, I'll kill him.'

But Clive was there again, unscathed, when the service man finally arrived. 'Cappuccino machine,' he said.

Daphne looked at him. 'I'm sorry?'

'You said there was something wrong with the cappuccino machine.'

'Oh yes.' Loose screw or not, the thing was still playing up. Daphne pointed. 'Over there.'

The repair man moved around behind the counter to examine the machine. Clive followed him. 'It's all right,' he told Daphne as he patted the man on the back. 'I'm sure he's done this thousands of times before. He's a fully qualified technician. We are in good hands.' He looked down at the man. 'You *will* warm your hands first, won't you?' The man gave Clive a puzzled stare as he moved back to the other side of the counter. 'I've got to be going,' Clive said to Daphne. 'I have an important call to make.'

'He's a doctor,' Daphne explained after he had gone.

The man shook his head in disbelief. 'They say it takes all kinds,' he said, thumping his fist on top of the cappuccino machine.

Daphne watched him in wide-eyed amazement as he pummelled the machine, on its top and against its sides. Yes, she thought drily, it certainly did take all kinds.

When Des Clarke walked into the shop about forty minutes later, the repair man had almost finished putting the machine together again. The cause of the trouble had been found; it was nestling in the palm of Daphne's hand.

'This gentleman has managed to fix the cappuccino machine,' she informed her husband.

'What was wrong with it?'

'This.' She extended her hand.

Des stared down at the small discoloured coin that lay in her palm. 'It's an old sixpence,' he observed.

'It took some finding,' the repair man told him as he wiped his hands on a piece of cloth. 'It was jamming the release valve.'

Des picked up the coin from Daphne's palm to examine it more closely. 'How did it get in there?'

Daphne knew the answer to that. 'This isn't just any old sixpence,' she said. 'When I took the shop over, the previous owners told me that they had taped the very first sixpence they earned to the back of the machine. Somehow it must have fallen off and got itself caught in the works. I'd forgotten all about it.'

Des was still studying the sixpenny piece that had caused all the trouble. 'Why would they do a thing like that?'

'For good luck, I suppose.'

Des smiled. 'Well, you've certainly had good luck since you took over this place.'

'What good luck?' Daphne queried.

'You married me, didn't you?'

'Yes.' She smiled at him fondly. 'That was the luckiest day of my life,' she said with feeling.

Des kissed her gently. 'That'll be fifty-five bucks, thanks,' the repair man said.

'What?' They stared at him.

'For the repair.'

'That's crazy!' Daphne exclaimed.

‘Fifty-five bucks?’ Des whistled softly. ‘For *sixpence*?’

The repair man glanced impatiently at his watch. ‘And another twenty-five if you argue on into the next half hour,’ he said.

With a quick glance at Des, Daphne hurried around the counter to the cash register. Des tossed the coin into the air and caught it. ‘I think I might just hang on to this,’ he said. ‘It might bring me good luck.’

‘It already has,’ Daphne remarked drily as she began counting out the money to pay the man.

Three

Scott Robinson had already convinced himself that he would fail his Maths exam. Oh, he had studied hard enough, and, as his father had tried to reassure him, there was no reason why he shouldn't make a good fist of it when the time came. 'Why don't you save the gloom and doom until after you've seen the paper?' he had suggested. 'You might get a pleasant surprise.'

There would be no pleasant surprises; the outcome was inevitable. 'I told you, Dad,' Scott had replied unhappily, 'I can't even remember the basic formulas. Without them, I'm a goner.'

On the morning of the exam, he did some last-minute cramming in the school grounds, his lips moving soundlessly as he tried desperately to memorise the elusive formulae. Earlier he had managed to reel them off to Nikki without a mistake. 'Give it a rest now,' she had advised him, 'or you'll only end up confusing yourself.'

He had been close to panic. 'My mind is just going to go blank once we're in there,' he had said in utter misery. 'I just know it will.'

A short time later, Nikki caught up with him as he moved away from the main school building. 'Scott, where are you going?'

'To get a drink,' he replied.

'Then you'd better hurry,' she said, 'or they'll lock you out of the exam.'

'Might be just as well,' he muttered as he moved past her.

There was something about his manner that worried Nikki. 'You're *not* going in, are you?' she queried.

'Yeah . . .'

By now Nikki's suspicions were truly aroused. 'You're up to something, Scott,' she said accusingly.

'Look . . .' He turned abruptly away from her. 'Back off, will you. I know what I'm doing.'

She stood squarely in front of him. 'I'm not going until you tell me what you're up to.'

He was looking away from her. 'It's better that you don't know, Nikki.'

'Don't know what?'

He was silent for a long moment. To Nikki, watching him closely, he seemed to be wrestling with some massive inner conflict. 'Look,' he said at last, 'the only way I'm going to pass these exams is . . . is if I take the answers in with me.'

Nikki was shocked. 'You're going to . . . *cheat*?'

Scott was looking increasingly uncomfortable. 'If I've got the formulae, I'll be okay.'

Nikki couldn't believe what she was hearing; this wasn't like Scott at all. 'But, Scott, that's crazy. There's no way you can smuggle a book in there for a start.'

'I won't need to do that.' Scott shook his head. 'I'm taking the answers in on my wrists.'

'I don't believe this!'

'You said it yourself.' He was obviously trying hard to defend his action. 'I *knew* the formulae. So, you really couldn't say it's cheating, could you? It's just a safety measure.'

'The supervisor won't think so if he catches you,' Nikki said. 'No one will.'

Scott sighed. 'I've got absolutely nothing to lose,' he said heavily. 'Not the way I've been going.'

It was madness. He would damage himself irrevocably if he went through with what he proposed. Nikki began to plead with him. 'Scott, please. Don't do it.'

'Just stay out of it, Nikki,' Scott said gruffly as he brushed past her.

Nikki stared after him in dismay as he walked quickly down the path beside the school building. She didn't know what to do. 'Scott, please,' she called, but he only quickened his steps. She was still staring after him when Charlene Mitchell, Jane Harris and Mike Young came up to her.

'What's the matter?' Mike asked. 'Your mind gone blank or something?'

Nikki shook her head grimly. '*Mine* hasn't.'

'Whose then?' Jane wanted to know.

Nikki noticed Sue Parker hovering near the corner of the school building. She kept her voice down. 'Scott's,' she answered. 'And not just blank. He's lost it completely.' She felt a sudden need to confide in them. Glancing past them to make sure Sue Parker was still out of earshot, she said, 'He's going to cheat in the exam.'

There was a gasp. They stared at her. 'He'll never get away with it,' Mike said in a horrified voice.

'They'll chuck him out.' Charlene turned away from them. 'I'm going to stop him.'

'No use,' Nikki said. 'He won't listen to you.'

'Yeah . . .' Charlene's face fell. Since their bust-up, Scott had been quite hostile towards her.

'Perhaps Mike could,' Nikki suggested.

Mike was still trying to come to terms with Nikki's revelation. He kept shaking his head. 'I can't believe he would do it,' he said uncomprehendingly. 'He's not that stupid.'

'No, he's desperate,' Nikki told him. 'He knows the stuff all right. It's just that he's lost confidence. He's got a lot on his mind at the moment.' She frowned at Charlene.

'Don't look at me,' Charlene said, backing way. '*I* wasn't the one who broke it off.'

'Maybe I *could* talk to him,' Mike suggested.

'Lots of luck,' Charlene remarked drily.

'I'll see if I can find him,' Mike said. 'You guys had better go on in. The exam will be starting shortly.'

As they made their way towards the classroom where they would be sitting for the examination, Nikki saw Sue Parker moving quickly along the path ahead of them. Thank God *she* didn't know anything about Scott's intentions, she thought. It would be disastrous if she did. 'Nosey' Parker was a girl who delighted in making trouble if she could.

'Cutting it a bit fine, aren't you?' Scott observed wrily as Mike hurried up to him.

Mike came straight to the point. 'I just want to stop you from doing something stupid.'

Scott tensed. 'Like what?'

Mike clutched his arm. 'Don't act so innocent, Scott,' he said urgently. 'I *know* what you're going to do.'

'What do you mean?' Scott was watching him closely.

'I mean that you're going to cheat at the exam.'

Angrily, Scott brushed his hand away. 'Damn Nikki and her big mouth,' he growled, his face reddening. 'I suppose the whole school knows about it by now.'

'She's worried about you, mate,' Mike said with a frown of concern. 'I mean, if you get busted you won't be able to sit for any more exams. You realise that, don't you?'

'I *won't* get busted,' Scott returned vehemently. 'I just wish that you and Nikki would get off my back. It's my life, and if I mess it up that's none of your business – okay?' Turning abruptly, he was about to storm away when an authoritative voice called to him from across the lawn.

'Just a minute, Scott.'

They waited apprehensively as Mr White, the school's Deputy Headmaster, crossed the grass towards them. 'Roll up your sleeves, will you, please,' he ordered Scott when he reached them.

With a thunderous glance at Mike, Scott unbuttoned his shirt sleeves and began to roll them up over his forearms. White took hold of one wrist and examined it briefly, then did the same with the other. Mike gave Scott a look that was compounded of both puzzlement and relief. Scott's expression was impassive. There was not a mark on either wrist.

'I'm sorry I had to do that, Scott,' White said as he released his wrist. 'I was obviously misinformed.'

'Yeah?' Scott's eyes were narrowed and hard. 'By whom?'

'I can't tell you that,' White said. 'You know that. But I will be speaking to the Headmaster about it.' He gestured towards the building behind them. 'Now you'd both better be getting off to the exam room.'

'But how am I supposed to concentrate?' Scott demanded. 'I mean, it was hard enough for me before.'

White smiled at him. 'I know you'll do your best, Scott,' he said. 'You always have in the past, and it shouldn't be any different now. Frankly, I didn't really think you were the type to do a thing like that, and I'm glad I was proved right. But I had to be absolutely certain, you see.'

Which didn't make Scott feel any less uptight. 'I know it's not your fault,' he said quietly. 'But I *am* starting to feel a bit shaky.'

'Just take a few deep breaths,' the master advised him. 'Walk slowly to the exam room, collect your thoughts and put this little incident right out of your head. You've got more important things to think about.' He patted Scott lightly and reassuringly on the shoulder. 'And good luck.'

'That's easy for him to say,' Scott said miserably when they were alone again.

'What happened?' Mike asked him. 'I thought you were going to be sprung.'

'Changed my mind, didn't I?'

'Thank God you did,' Mike said with a chuckle, then shook his head. 'But Nikki said . . .'

'What would *she* know?' Then Scott's voice softened. 'I was going to,' he said, 'but when it came to the crunch I couldn't go through with it. I tried to convince myself that it wasn't cheating, but no matter how you looked at it that's just what it was.'

Mike was grinning broadly at him. 'Good old Robinson honesty, eh?'

'I guess so.' Scott's face hardened again. 'But just wait till I catch the person who dobbed me in,' he vowed darkly.

He didn't catch up with Nikki again until the ordeal of the exam was over. 'Okay,' he demanded savagely. 'Who did you shoot off your big mouth to?'

'Well, there was Mike . . .'

'I know about Mike. Who else?'

Knowing how he felt about her, Nikki was reluctant to mention Charlene. 'What difference does it make? You didn't cheat.'

'That's not the point. Someone put me in with Whitey. If it wasn't you, I want to know who else knew about it.'

'Come on, Scott,' Jane said. 'We wouldn't dob on you.'

'Oh no?' Scott looked at her doubtfully. 'Well, how did he find out about it?' No one said anything; there was no answer to that. Scott persisted. 'I mean, it's typical of Nikki to open her mouth in front of the whole school.'

'Oh?' Nikki glared at him. 'Do you *really* think I would want everyone in the school to know my cousin is a cheat?' she challenged him.

Mike stepped in to keep the peace. 'Fighting about it is not going to help,' he said sharply. 'Look Scott, Nikki told me, Jane and Charlene – no one else.'

'Charlene?' Scott seized on the name. 'Why didn't you tell me before?'

'Charlene would be the last one to dob anyone in,' Jane said.

Scott glanced around the school yard. 'Where is she then?'

Mike shrugged. 'We don't know.'

'She's gone home,' Nikki said. 'She's probably sick of being around a whinger like you.'

'More like a guilty conscience you mean,' Scott muttered.

'You've got it all wrong, Scott. She wouldn't tell Mister White.'

'Wouldn't she?' Scott swung angrily away. 'We'll find out then.'

'Mike, stop him,' Nikki said urgently as Scott began to stride away from the group.

'Guess I would have more trouble stopping a semi-trailer,' Mike said ruefully. He thought for a moment.

'Maybe I should talk to Mister White. He might tell me who it was.'

'We may as well go to the coffee shop and wait,' Nikki suggested.

'Okay.' Jane turned to Mike. 'Tell us when you find out.'

'I will,' Mike promised as he headed back towards the school building.

Charlene had just made herself a sandwich and was preparing some chocolate milk when Scott burst into the Ramsay kitchen through the back door. 'Thanks, Charlene,' he growled. 'Thanks a lot.'

Charlene quickly recovered from her surprise. 'Come in, why don't you?'

'You're lucky I didn't break the door down.'

'Well, make sure you open it on the way out then.'

As she made to move past him, he grabbed her arm. 'Hey, don't walk away from me.'

'Watch it, you idiot!' Angrily, she wrenched herself free. 'What the hell are you on about, anyway?'

'You. Putting me in to Mister White. Oh, come on, Charlene. As if you didn't know.'

'You're a wombat, Scott.'

'Oh yeah? Then how did Whitey know I was going to cheat?'

Charlene looked at him in sudden concern. 'You were caught?'

'No. I didn't go through with it in the end.'

'Then what's all the fuss about?'

'I thought I could trust my friends,' Scott said bitterly. 'Not have them blabbing off to the teachers.'

'You've been acting like a pig for weeks, Scott,' Charlene said tartly. 'But this time you've gone right over the top. The way you've been carrying on, you don't deserve to pass.'

'There, you've just said it,' Scott cried in bitter triumph. 'I *knew* you must have done it.'

Charlene was beginning to lose her temper. 'Get real, Scott. Do you *honestly* think I would report you? Or anyone else for that matter?' She shook her head. 'I've been in more trouble than the lot of you put together.'

Scott still wasn't convinced. 'Charlene, nobody else *could* have done it.'

'Oh yes, they could,' a voice said quietly behind him.

Scott spun round to face Mike Young, who had just entered through the open back door. 'Stay out of it!' he snapped.

'No, don't,' Charlene urged. 'What do you mean, Mike?'

Mike closed the door behind him. 'It was Sue Parker,' he said solemnly.

'That figures,' Charlene remarked drily. 'That would be typical of her.'

'Oh . . . right.' Scott regarded her coldly. 'And I suppose a little birdie told *her*.'

'Actually, it was more like a galah, Scott,' Mike said. '*You* told her. She heard you talking to Nikki.'

'There you go,' Charlene said with a quick smile. '*I* think you're a wombat and Mike thinks you're a galah.'

Scott ignored her; he glared at Mike. 'I suppose she just broke down and confessed – did she?'

'No, she didn't,' Mike said firmly. 'I went to see Whitey and he let it slip that the Principal was looking into it. So I hung around outside the office to see who came out.' He eyed Scott steadily. 'I think you should apologise to Charlene.' He opened the door. 'Now I'd better go. I've got an exam this afternoon.'

'Don't bother apologising,' Charlene snapped after Mike had gone. 'Just get out.'

'Yeah, well . . .' Scott shifted uncomfortably. 'You can't blame me for thinking it was you,' he muttered.

'Can't I?' She blazed at him. 'If *that's* what you think of me,' she cried, 'I never want to see you again.' Picking up her sandwich and chocolate milk, she stormed out of the room. 'Starting right now.'

Scott stared unhappily after her, then, with a shrug, made for the door.

Four

Susan needed brightening up. 'Hey, come on,' Clive said encouragingly. 'Things can't be that bad.'

Susan sighed and shook her head sorrowfully. 'Have you ever tried spending a lot of time with someone you love – and all that someone wants to be is just a good friend?'

Clive knew exactly what it was like; it was how he was spending all his time these days. 'Yes,' he murmured. 'It can be tough.' Then he rallied. 'But you can handle it. Remember how much trouble you had getting that job in the first place?'

Not easy at all. A young, unmarried mother who desperately had to make ends meet. 'If I didn't remember, I would have left already,' Susan said, staring down at her coffee cup. 'But, frankly, Clive, it's just impossible . . .'

Reaching across the table, he gently patted her hand. 'Just a little time – that's all you need. Everything gets easier with time.'

'I suppose.' She smiled wanly up at him.

'That's the spirit.' Clive beamed back at her. He had a thought. 'Listen, how about we go out tonight? Paint the town green?'

She looked puzzled. 'Shouldn't that be red?'

Clive touched his unruly mop of bright ginger hair. 'When you've got hair my colour,' he told her, 'you look for something different.'

She laughed – and Clive was grateful; he had managed to take her mind of Paul Robinson for the time being at least. 'Oh, Clive, I appreciate what you're trying to do, but I'm such lousy company. Will it be all right if we just have dinner at home?'

'Sure. Sam and I can talk between ourselves. But on one condition – that we dress up for dinner.'

'Okay.' She smiled at him more warmly. 'You're on.'

After Susan had returned to the office to suffer yet a few more hours of Paul Robinson's indifference towards her, Clive spent the afternoon making the house look more festive by stringing up streamers and balloons, and even, from the centre of the ceiling, a small glitter dome he had unearthed from among the jumble in one of the cupboards.

'Oh, Clive, this looks wonderful,' Susan exclaimed as she arrived that evening.

'Sam and I are dressed for dinner,' Clive called from upstairs, then, with a fanfare blown on a toy bugle, he carried the baby down to her. They were both wearing clown costumes. Clive paddled along on outsize shoes. Susan laughed when she saw them – Clive and his miniature replica.

'You didn't say anything about clowning around.'

Clive made a face at the baby. 'She's pinching our gags, Sam,' he said.

'What am I going to be?' Susan asked.

'How about the daring young girl on the flying trapeze?' Clive suggested.

'No way. I'm petrified of heights.'

'That's okay. Our trapeze is built especially for people like you.' He pointed to a corner of the living room where he had set up a trapeze that was barely a foot from the floor.

'Doctor Gibbons, you are your own best medicine.'

'You're too kind, madam.' Clive bowed from the waist. 'Now upstairs with you. Your costume is on your bed – and it's okay. You're a clown, not an acrobat.'

She was laughing happily. 'Clive, you're adorable,' she said, heading for the stairs. 'Crazy but adorable.'

Clive grinned at the baby in his arms. 'I think that means she likes me,' he said, tickling him under the chin and making him gurgle. 'Hey, Sam? Right or wrong?'

Susan looked adorable with her false nose. 'Didn't we meet once on the back of a cereal packet?' Clive asked her as she reached the foot of the stairs.

She smiled a little self-consciously. 'I feel really ridiculous.'

'*You* feel ridiculous.' With an effort, Clive raised one of his gigantic shoes from the floor. 'Imagine going to a chiropodist in shoes like these. He'd run a mile.' He lowered his foot again. 'Now we can eat, or we can throw it around the room. Take your pick.'

Sam's bassinet was festooned with balloons and streamers. Susan glanced across at the tiny clown that was lying peacefully inside it. 'I'd better fix some juice for Sam,' she said. 'He might get thirsty later.'

'No sooner said than done.' Clive produced a bottle from behind his back. 'The hand is quicker than the eye.' He moved across to the bassinet and held the bottle out above it. 'Orange juice, kid. You'll love it. A regular three-ring citrus.'

'Oh, stop it,' Susan groaned. 'Feed me.'

Clive gestured grandly to the table which had already been set for dinner. 'First seat on the aisle. Best seat in the house.' He stood beside Susan at the table with his arm around her as he addressed an imaginary crowd. 'Now, ladies and gentlemen . . . the young at heart . . . the greatest show on earth. You've read the book, you've seen the movie . . .' he gestured to the dishes on the table '. . . now eat the menu.'

Susan was gradually entering the spirit of the occasion. She peered down at the food. 'Let me guess. Barnum and Bailey burgers?'

'You're warm. And so are the burgers.' Clive indicated the other dishes. 'High-wire hotdogs, lion-tamer lasagna – and trapizza.' He sat down opposite her. 'And good wine for a funny lady.'

'I'm not very funny,' Susan said. 'I don't know any jokes.'

'You know *me*.' Clive sounded pained.

'Yes, you.' Susan helped herself to lasagna while Clive poured the wine. She raised a forkful to her mouth, but the false nose was in the way. 'Oh dear, I don't think it's going to work,' she said, lowering the fork.

'So why do you think the good Lord gave us rubber bands?' Clive asked her.

'Oh yes, I see . . .' Pulling the false nose clear of her face, she downed the forkful of lasanga. 'Very good.'

Suddenly, as she was bringing another forkful of lasagna up to her mouth, the lights went out and the music stopped. The lasagna slid off the end of her fork onto her lap. 'Oops.'

'Not to worry. Not to worry.' Clive was floundering about on his outsized feet. He opened a cupboard door and rummaged for a moment. 'Ah, got it,' he said, coming back to the table. 'All we have to do is rub two sticks together.'

The room wasn't completely dark; some moonlight filtered in through the curtains. Susan had retrieved the lump of lasagna from her lap. Clive was lighting the candles in the candelabra he had brought back to the table.

'Where did you get that? It's awful.'

'Yes, a remarkable piece of junk.' Clive lit the last candle. 'Murphy's Op-Shop, Transylvania. Mail order.'

'Clive, you planned this,' Susan said.

'What? The black-out?' Clive shook his head. 'I wish I did, but the whole street's out.'

'No lights, no music. I'm sorry about your circus.'

From the bassinet, Sam began to cry. 'The circus can wait,' Clive said. 'Right now, we're in a cave, on the edge of a primeval forest. The tom-toms are beating in the darkness, the natives are getting restless – and the lasagna is getting cold . . .'

Clive was refilling the wine glasses when Susan came back downstairs after putting Sam to bed by candlelight. 'Any problems?' he asked, putting the bottle down.

'Curled up like a lamb.' Susan sighed as she sat down again. 'Sometimes I wouldn't mind being Sam.'

'Best time of your life,' Clive agreed. 'It's when you let go of Mum's hand and step out into the big wide world that it gets rough. You scrape your knee, you stub your toe – then you strike the real problems. Other people.'

The candles flickered slightly on the table between them. 'Especially the ones you fall in love with,' Susan murmured sadly.

Clive stood up. 'Come on, let's sit over on the sofa,' he suggested, picking up their glasses. 'We'll be more comfortable.'

'All right.'

Beside her on the sofa, he raised his glass and smiled at her in the moonlight. 'It's not every day I get a chance to share a glass of moonlight with the most beautiful girl in the world,' he said tenderly.

'You don't mean that.'

'I may joke,' he said seriously, 'but I never lie.'

'That's why you get hurt; you give too much. You should be more like Paul.' Now there was bitterness in her voice. 'He just takes. No strings, no commitments . . .'

'He's a bore.'

'Life's not very fair, is it?' Susan's thoughts were obviously far away. 'I *know* what Paul is like, but I keep on letting him hurt me.'

'I wish I could do something about that,' Clive said earnestly.

Her voice was unsteady; she was on the verge of tears. 'I'm sorry, Clive. You've gone to so much trouble, and I'm ruining it.'

'That's okay.' He placed a comforting arm around her shoulders. 'Friend, yeah?'

Susan relaxed against him. 'My very best friend.'

He held her lovingly in his arms. The combined moonlight and candlelight contributed to a soft and romantic atmosphere. Clive's thoughts were wistful. If only she didn't love Paul so much; if only she could realise how much he loved her; if only . . . Outside, the street lights came on. 'Power must be back on,' he observed. 'Do you want me to turn the lights back on? I switched them off after the black-out. I didn't want to risk a fuse.'

She was still nestling against him. 'No, it's okay.'

Clive was pleased. 'Much nicer without them.'

'You know, Clive,' Susan said distantly, 'I was a bit like Paul once. I thought I could just take what I wanted from life. And then I had Sam. Now, I want him to have a father who loves him, and a happy home where he can grow up. I don't want anything for myself, except . . .' she sighed '. . . except the one thing I *can't* have.'

'Maybe you should give Paul a little more time,' Clive suggested.

'Time's not going to change anything.' Susan shook her head. 'It's finished.' She sat up and turned to face Clive who, in the moonlight, could see that her cheeks were glistening. 'Tell me, Clive, how do you fall out of love with someone?'

'You find someone else,' he replied simply.

'Yes . . . maybe . . .' She was staring at him intently, her eyes wide and shining, her full lips slightly parted.

Very gently, before he quite realised what he was doing, Clive kissed the tears from her cheeks, then drew back. It wasn't right; it wasn't fair to her.

But then she was reaching for him, hungrily, desperately, her lips seeking his – and with a surge of joy, Clive at last surrendered to the feelings that had been bottled up inside him for so long.

•

Clive was quite light-headed as he prepared breakfast the following morning. He was singing as he flitted happily about the kitchen. He bobbed fondly over little Sam's bassinet as he waited for Susan to come downstairs. He was a man very definitely in love.

'You'd better get used to the good life, Sammy,' he joyfully told the baby. 'The best house, the best education, a BMX bike. But don't ask me about women. That's one mystery you'll have to figure out for yourself.' He waltzed away to the stove to check the temperature of the baby's bottle. 'One day, when you fall in love, I'll tell you how I fell in love with your Mum – and you're not going to believe it.' He brought the baby's bottle back to the bassinet. 'Of course I'll love you, and protect you – and tell you off if you do the wrong thing. I mean, that's what fathers are supposed to do, aren't they?' Suddenly becoming aware that Susan was standing in the doorway, watching him, he rushed across to greet her. 'Good morning.' Slipping his arms around her, he kissed her. 'Did I tell you that you look beautiful by moonlight?'

She seemed rather preoccupied this morning, a little withdrawn. 'Clive . . .'

'Yes, I know. I'm biased.'

The toast was burning. Hurrying across the room, Clive plucked it out of the toaster. 'I'm sorry I was so maudlin last night,' Susan said. 'You went to so much trouble.'

Clive was waving away the smoke from the burning toast. 'Hey, who *can* you talk to if you can't talk to me?' He became serious. 'Anyway, I made myself a promise this morning. I promised that there would be no more tears for this family. We're going to set new records on the happiness scale.'

Susan didn't seem to have much appetite this morning. Clive placed a glass of orange juice in front of her as she sat down at the table. 'I've got a surprise for you,' he announced cheerfully.

'I don't think I'm up to surprises.' She sipped her drink.

'You'll like this one.' Clive had spent half the night lying awake and thinking about it. 'Once I've got the loan to buy this place, I'm putting half of it in your name.'

'Oh, Clive.' She was clearly shocked by his announcement. She replaced the glass on the table.

'Now I don't want any arguments.' Clive waved a forestalling finger in front of her. 'I want you and Sam to feel secure – and this is the best way.'

'But, Clive, you can't do that.' She was staring up at him in dismay.

Clive had expected an argument, but he had already made up his mind; it was the least he could do for the woman he loved. 'Don't worry about it,' he said lightly. 'Don't give it another thought.'

'But, Clive . . .'

'I've made up my mind.'

'Clive, we have to talk.'

'Do you want more orange juice?'

'A serious talk.'

'Good idea. We haven't have a serious talk for ages.' He moved around the kitchen, busying himself, keeping his tone light, trying to stave off the inevitable. 'And with the world falling apart, the least we can do is be a bit intense. So where would you like to start? The Middle East? The problem of international terrorism? Mrs Thatcher?'

'How about Ramsay Street?'

'Nah . . .' Clive shook his head. 'That's a bit ordinary. How about . . . let me think . . . the breeding grounds of the gooney bird?'

'Clive . . .' Susan was becoming exasperated.

'No?' He raised his eyebrows. 'Too serious?'

'We'll have to talk sooner or later.'

'We *are* talking.'

'No, we're not.'

'Yes, we are.'

'Look, Clive, this can't wait any longer.'

'Not even for toast?'

'Not even for toast.'

Clive sighed; he sensed what was coming. 'Okay, shoot.'

'I know you're in love with me, Clive,' Susan said quietly across the breakfast table. 'The trouble is, I don't feel the same way about you.'

It was out – the devastating truth. Perhaps he had really known it all along. 'But last night . . .'

'It was a mistake. It was all my fault. I just felt so alone. But after Paul . . . the way he's been . . . I just wanted to be with someone who cared about me.'

Clive felt totally deflated. He stared bleakly at the woman he loved. 'You're still in love with him, aren't you?'

Susan shrugged helplessly. 'I'm an idiot, I guess.'

'I guess.' Clive tried to make light of it. 'Oh . . . shall I get that toast now?'

She stopped him as he was about to move away from the table. She smiled up at him a little shakily. 'Oh, Clive, you're a very, very special person . . . wonderful person. And if I could choose who to fall in love with – well, you would be at the top of the list. But things don't work that way.'

No, they certainly did not, Clive thought sadly. If she could choose who to fall in love with. 'No, I guess not,' he murmured.

Reaching across the table, she took his hand. 'I wish it was different, but it's not. There's no use pretending otherwise.'

There was a long and painful silence. Clive was the first to speak. 'Is that it?'

She released his hand. 'I would have thought that was enough.'

Clive raised his glass of orange juice. 'Cheers,' he said, making an effort to be bright, not to show how deeply wounded he was. 'You finally got to say it.' He drank some of his juice. 'What happens now?'

'I don't know.' Susan was close to tears.

'Well, I suppose we'll have to decide.'

'We'll have to do something.'

'But . . .' Clive suddenly blurted it out. 'Can't you *ever* love me?'

'I don't know.' Susan shook her head sorrowfully. 'I've asked myself that so many times, and I just don't know the answer. Perhaps in time . . .' She made a visible effort to pull herself together. 'But I can't promise anything.'

'Are you moving out with Sam?'

'Do you want us to?'

She and the baby had walked into his life; they had completely transformed it. If they were to go now . . . He shook his head and studied her miserably across the table. 'I *do* love you, Susan,' he said quietly. 'And if there's a chance that you might . . . learn to love me, even if it's a million to one chance, then I want you to stay.'

'Are you sure?' Her eyes were brimming.

'Of course I'm sure.' God, she looked beautiful in her dressing gown and with her hair all tousled, her eyes moist and slightly puffy with sleep. He smiled hopefully. 'Want to give it a go? See what happens?'

'I'm not promising anything,' Susan said in a small voice. 'I can't do that. But . . .' her lips were trembling a little as she tried to smile back at him '. . . I'm willing to stay – give it a go.'

The relief surged powerfully through Clive. He knew where he stood now – and there was still hope. Taking her hand, he kissed it fervently. 'That's all I can ever ask,' he said.

Five

Eileen Clarke was speechless. She was literally speechless. She had screamed once, then when she tried to scream again all she had been able to manage was a husky croak, which was awful enough, right on the eve of the concert she had arranged to give at the Senior Citizens' Hall. In many ways, when she had calmed down a little and had time to think about it, it was worse than having her bag snatched in broad daylight by a hoodlum on a motor-bike.

There was a commotion at the bank that afternoon when Daphne Clarke arrived to make a deposit. 'We've just had a thief in here,' Des told her.

Daphne looked at her husband in alarm. 'A bank robber?'

Des smiled and shook his head. 'The thief who stole Mum's handbag,' he explained. 'She tried to withdraw cash from Mum's account.'

'You mean the guy on the motor-bike was a *girl*?'

'Using the term loosely' Des said with a nod. 'We tried to stall her, but she became suspicious. Shane chased after her.'

'That's really bright,' Daphne observed. 'Coming in here to try and pass herself off as the bank manager's mother.'

'Yes, wasn't it?'

There were sounds of a scuffle from outside. 'Let me go!' a girl's voice cried. 'Take your hands off me, or I'll do you for assault.'

Then Shane Ramsay was bringing the struggling girl into the bank. He hauled her across to where Des and Daphne were standing. Daphne studied her curiously; she had seen the girl before somewhere.

'She's all yours, Des,' Shane said.

Her face contorted with anger, the girl was still struggling to free herself from Shane. She swore. 'That's enough,' Des crisply admonished her. 'You've got some explaining to do.'

'Rack off.' The girl glared defiantly at Des.

'That attitude won't help you at all,' Des said.

She was quite a pretty girl. Daphne suddenly remembered where she had seen her before. 'You're Kelly, aren't you? Kelly Morgan? You used to come to the coffee shop.'

'Did I?' the girl returned sullenly.

'You're in a lot of trouble, young lady,' Des said firmly.

'So?' She jeered at him. 'You don't scare me.'

'Then maybe the police will. They'll be here soon.'

Now, suddenly, the girl wasn't quite so defiant. Watching her closely, Daphne noticed the small crack that had appeared in her armour. 'Well . . . I'll tell them you're making it all up.'

'I don't care *what* you tell them,' Des said, 'as long as they take you off my hands.'

Now the girl was beginning to look frightened. 'Please . . .' An imploring expression came into her eyes. 'I'll give it all back . . . all the stuff I took. I only did it because I was desperate. Don't bring the cops into it, please!' She turned to Daphne who was already beginning to feel a little sorry for her. 'Look, I've been done before. They'll put me away this time.'

Daphne glanced at Des whose expression remained implacable. 'It's not up to me, Kelly,' she said awkwardly.

'I'm only seventeen,' she pleaded. 'I don't want to go to gaol.'

'You should have thought about that,' Des said sternly, 'before you started snatching handbags from poor defenceless little old ladies.'

Daphne and Shane exchanged a surprised glance. Eileen? Poor, defenceless and little? 'I don't think she'd really like to be described that way, Des,' Daphne remarked.

'That's not the point.' Des waved the irrelevancy brusquely away. 'You can complain all you like,' he said to Kelly, 'but the police are coming, and that's all there is to it.'

By the time the police arrived, Daphne was quite concerned about the girl. She wasn't really as hard as she made herself seem; she was very young, very vulnerable – and yes, perhaps she really had been desperate enough to do what she had done. 'Why don't you ring your Mum?' she suggested, while Des was explaining what had happened to the two uniformed policemen. 'She'll be worried about you.'

Kelly's lips curled derisively. 'The only thing *she's* worried about is where the next beer's coming from.'

Daphne sighed. 'I'm sure she'd help if she knew you were in trouble,' she said.

'She couldn't care less,' Kelly said with a toss of her head. 'Besides, she has already kicked me out. She said she doesn't want to have anything more to do with me.'

'But . . .' Daphne wasn't finding this easy. 'Well,

lots of mothers say that, but they don't usually mean it.'

'You don't know mine,' Kelly muttered.

Daphne was determined to help the girl in any way she could. 'Why don't *I* talk to her?' she suggested. 'I think you should at least give her the *chance* of helping you.'

'You'll be wasting your time.'

'I'd still like to try.'

'Suit yourself.' Kelly shrugged offhandedly. 'Only don't bother trying her at home because she'll be at the pub.'

It was just as Kelly had predicted; her mother, when Daphne sought her out in the back bar of the local pub, more than a little drunk and surrounded by cigarette smoke, beer fumes and noisy chatter, couldn't have cared less about Kelly. In fact, she became quite hostile. Kelly could rot in hell as far as she was concerned. On her way home, Daphne came to a decision.

'I've decided to bail her out myself,' she announced.

'You *what*?' Des's eyes widened in amazement. Eileen, who was staying with them until she recovered from the shock of losing her voice and her handbag, furiously scribbled something on the notepad through which all her utterances now had to be channelled until such time as her voice was restored to her.

'No one else cares about her,' Daphne said.

Eileen held up the pad so Daphne could see what she had written. On it was scrawled the word 'Traitor'.

'I need two hundred dollars,' Daphne told Des.

'You're joking.' Des was staring at her in disbelief. 'I wouldn't spend a cent on that girl after what she did to Mum. Beides, I don't have two hundred bucks on me.'

Daphne was desperately seeking a straw to clutch. 'I've got to do *something*,' she said urgently. 'Otherwise she'll spend the whole weekend in gaol.' Glaring fiercely at her, Eileen was still holding up the notepad. 'Eileen, I know she's done the wrong thing,' Daphne said. 'But that doesn't stop me feeling sorry for her.'

Rising to her feet, Eileen stalked huffily out of the room. 'I don't blame her, Daph,' Des said. 'I mean, you seem to be more concerned with Kelly than what actually happened to Mum.'

'It isn't that, Des,' Daphne said with a helpless shake of her head. 'It's just that I have a good reason for being worried about Kelly.'

'Why don't you tell me about it?'

It wasn't until after dinner that night that she did tell him. It had been a rather strained affair, with Daphne doing her best to make conversation with Eileen while the older woman just sat there in an accusing silence. 'I'm trying to make it up with her,' Daphne complained to Des when Eileen abruptly took from her the plates she had been gathering up from the table and carried them out into the kitchen, 'but she just won't let me.'

'You've got to see it from her point of view,' Des said reasonably. 'I mean, here you are, trying to raise bail for someone who robbed your own mother-in-law.'

'Oh, it's far more complicated than that.' Daphne began to explain what it was that worried her so much about Kelly. 'When she used to come into the coffee shop, it was obvious that she was a kid who was just drifting. I tried to make friends with her, to get through to her in some way. Then she just stopped coming.'

'Probably out stripping cars or something,' Des snorted.

'All the more reason why we should try. It doesn't stop me wanting to help her.'

She could see that he was becoming annoyed with her. 'Daphne, if you hand over that two hundred dollars, she'll just shoot through and you'll never see that money again.'

'That's not the point.'

'Then what *is* the point?'

Daphne was silent for a moment; the memory was still painful for her. 'When I was counselling,' she said at last, 'I met a girl who was a lot like Kelly. Just like her – same background, everything. She ended up in gaol . . . and later I learned that she had been killed. In a riot.' She looked at her husband beseechingly. 'Gaols are terrible places, Des. Terrible things happen there.'

'That still doesn't mean you should feel responsible for Kelly.'

'I can't help it. That's the way I feel.'

'But she *deserves* to be in gaol.'

She wasn't getting through to him – and that saddened her deeply.

In the end, she borrowed the money from the coffee shop takings. She was down at the police station early the following morning. The formalities were quite simple. 'Thanks for getting me out, Daphne,' Kelly said as they emerged from the station. She gave a careless wave and turned in the opposite direction. 'See you in court.'

'Wait a minute.' Catching up with her, Daphne grabbed her arm. 'You're coming home with me.'

Kelly was looking quite bedraggled after her night in the cell. She eyed Daphne with suspicion. 'What for?' she demanded.

'You're staying with me until you go to court.'

'What's the matter?' She was sneering at Daphne.

'Don't you reckon I'll turn up? Frightened you'll lose your money?'

'Could be,' Daphne replied evenly. 'Anyway, where else can you go?'

'I can look after myself,' Kelly returned defiantly.

They faced each other squarely on the almost deserted street.

'Yes,' Daphne said, 'and if you get into any more trouble before you appear in court there'll be no way of keeping you out of gaol.'

Kelly's gaze faltered; she seemed to flinch. Obviously her night in the cell hadn't been a particularly pleasant experience for her.

Daphne presented her with a choice. 'Now, at my place, you've got a roof over your head, a bed to sleep in, and food on the table. What's wrong with that?'

Kelly thought about that. 'Depends on what sort of strings are attached.'

'No strings,' Daphne assured her. 'I just want you to keep your nose clean.'

If Kelly was tempted, and Daphne thought she was, she still had an objection to raise. 'The trouble with people like you is that you always expect something in return.'

'All I want to do is help. I don't want anything from you.'

'Yeah, sure.' Kelly's expression was sceptical. 'I've met your type of do-gooder before. You're all the same.'

Daphne decided it was time to take a tougher line with the girl. 'I put up the money for your bail,' she crisply reminded her, 'and as far as I'm concerned that makes me responsible for you. I want you where I can keep an eye on you.' She spoke firmly in a tone that would brook no opposition. 'You're coming home with me – is that clear?'

Kelly stared at her unwaveringly for a long moment, then with a slow smile, shrugged her shoulders. 'It's your funeral,' she said.

As they pulled up outside Daphne's house, she noticed a brand new red car in the Robinson driveway next door. 'What do you think of it?' Paul Robinson gestured proudly towards the car.

'I like the colour.'

'That's all you women think about.'

Daphne laughed. 'Sexist.'

Scott and Lucy Robinson were also standing beside Paul's new car. Scott saw Kelly staring at the car in open admiration. 'Kelly Morgan, isn't it?' he asked, approaching her.

'Oh yes.' Daphne stepped in to make the introductions. 'Kelly, these are the Robinsons. The little one is Lucy. You probably remember Paul and Scott from school.'

'Been a while since I was there,' Kelly remarked unenthusiastically.

'Couple of years I'd say,' Scott said.

'Probably.' Kelly's eyes were drawn back to the shining new car. 'Nice set of wheels,' she observed.

'It should do me for a while,' Paul said easily.

'Yeah.' Kelly didn't sound impressed. 'Until the ashtrays are full, anyway.' She turned away.

'I'll see you later,' Daphne said awkwardly as she began to follow Kelly. 'Great car, Paul.'

Eileen was gradually recovering her voice; it was still hardly more than a croak which rose alarmingly when she realised what Daphne had done. 'I refuse to spend a single night under the same roof as this . . . creature.'

'Careful, Mum,' Des warned her. 'You'll ruin your voice altogether.'

Daphne turned to him. 'Des, will you show Kelly the spare room,' she said.

Eileen was aghast; outrage was being heaped on outrage. 'But my things are in there,' she exclaimed. She pleaded with her son. 'Desmond, you *can't* expect me to share my room with a . . . a mad dog.'

'Your voice, Mum,' Des warned her again.

'We've only got the one spare bedroom,' Daphne reminded her.

Now it was Kelly's turn to object. 'I'm not sharing with her,' she said flatly.

Daphne glared at her. 'Kelly, will you please go with Des,' she commanded fiercely.

Kelly hesitated, then with a shrug followed Des out into the hall. Daphne turned back to her mother-in-law. 'We'll sort it all out,' she said. 'While you're here she can sleep on the sofa.' When Eileen made a sound of disgust, Daphne tried to make her see reason. 'She's got nowhere else to go, Eileen. She's been sleeping in doorways and on park benches.'

'With all the money she's been stealing,' Eileen said huffily, 'I would have thought she could afford a hotel.'

'She can barely afford to feed herself,' Daphne said in growing exasperation. 'Look . . .' She sighed; it was never easy to get through to her mother-in-law. 'I intend to supervise her until her appearance in court. After that, depending on what happens, we'll review the situation.'

'And what *I* hope will happen,' Eileen croaked, 'is that she receives a good stiff gaol sentence. That'll wake her up to herself.'

'I think a little more care and consideration will do more good.' Daphne spoke softly but vehemently. 'And that's what I intend to give her.' Once again she began to plead for reason to prevail. 'Eileen, these kids don't get a chance. It's up to us to give them one when we can.'

'Very well, Daphne.' Eileen's voice was pained. 'You'll obviously do what you think is fit – and I'm only destroying what is left of my voice by trying.' She rose to her feet with impressive dignity. 'I shall be moving back to my flat this afternoon.' She looked sorrowfully at the daughter-in-law who was treating her so shabbily. 'I just want you to know that I have been cut to the quick.' She drew herself up to her full height and pointed an accusing finger. 'You took that little law-breaker's side, and against your own mother-in-law.' She sighed deeply and clutched her ample bosom. 'It's like a knife in my heart. Or should I say in my back?' With that parting thrust she left the room.

Daphne was discussing the situation with Des when Kelly came back into the living room. 'No one wants me here, do they?' she said, after Daphne had explained to her that Eileen would probably be leaving that afternoon.

'I do.' Daphne gave her an encouraging smile.

Kelly turned to Des. 'What about you?'

'Well . . .' Des shrugged half-heartedly. 'It's okay with me.'

'No, it's not.' Kelly scowled at him. 'Look, I'm not an idiot,' she said harshly. 'I know you don't want me here – and I don't want to be here, either.' She swung back to face Daphne. 'All you're interested in is your bail money.' She ran out of the room. A moment later the front door slammed.

'It's going to be a long haul, Daph,' Des said with a sigh. 'I don't think she *wants* to be cared for.'

'Of course she does,' Daphne insisted. 'She's just acting that way because she has been hurt. She feels unloved and unwanted. It's a lousy way to feel. I know. I've felt that way myself.'

Sitting beside her on the sofa, Des placed his arm around her and gave her a fond hug. 'There's no need for you to feel that way now.'

Daphne smiled gratefully back at him. 'Yes, I know.'

He kissed her. 'Okay, Daph,' he said. 'I'm right behind you. All the way.'

'Thanks.' Daphne gently disengaged herself from the embrace and stood up. 'I'd better go and see what's happened to her.'

She was just opening the front door when she heard a car starting up in the driveway next door. As she stepped out on to the porch she saw Paul Robinson's new car backing out on to the street. Suddenly, to her horror, she realised that it wasn't Paul behind the wheel but Kelly. She began running towards the street. 'Kelly!' she yelled at the top of her voice. 'Kelly, stop!' But the car was already heading along the street, away from her. In open-mouthed dismay. she stared after it until it was out of sight, then sprinted across the lawn to the Robinson house.

Helen Daniels was alone in the house. Daphne was quite beside herself with rage and worry as she burst in through the kitchen door. 'The little thief!' she cried. 'That's all she is.'

Helen had just been making out a shopping list. 'What's wrong?' she asked, looking up from the table with a worried frown.

'I trusted her.'

'Daphne, what is it?'

'Kelly has taken Paul's car.'

'His new car?' Helen rose to her feet. 'He'll be furious.'

Paul was out with Scott who had borrowed Clive

Gibbons' old bomb of a car so that Paul could give him a driving lesson rather than risk anything happening to his new acquisition. 'I wish I knew how we're going to break the news to him,' Helen said with a sigh.

'I'll tell him,' Daphne said bitterly. 'It's my responsibility.' She moved across to the telephone. 'Don't worry, Helen. Paul will get his car back. Kelly's not getting away with it this time.' She picked up the receiver. 'I'm calling the police.'

'He will if you don't,' Helen remarked.

'Des and Eileen were right.' Daphne began to dial. 'I've been an idiot.'

'I heard you were having your problems,' Helen said. 'I heard all about it from Madge Mitchell. She heard all about it from Eileen.'

'So I suppose by now it's all around the neighbourhood that I've betrayed my mother-in-law.' Eileen would make sure of that.

'You were just trying to help the girl. No one can blame you for that.'

The number was ringing. A voice answered. 'I'd like to report a stolen car,' Daphne said.

'Hang up.' Helen Daniels was looking out the window.

'Just a minute,' Daphne said uncertainly into the mouthpiece.

'I think she's back,' Helen said.

'Sorry, false alarm.' Hurriedly, Daphne replaced the receiver. 'I'll kill her,' she cried as she dashed to the door.

The car had barely come to a halt on the sloping driveway when Daphne yanked the door open, reached in, and grabbed hold of Kelly's arm. 'Out!' she ordered.

'Let go,' Kelly yelped. 'You're hurting me.'

Daphne dragged her out of the car. 'I haven't even started yet.'

When Kelly was out of the car, she faced Daphne with defiance. 'What's wrong with you?' she demanded. 'I only took it for a ride.' She gestured to the car behind her. 'I brought it back, didn't I?'

Damn her cheek! Daphne only just managed to restrain herself from striking the girl. 'Oh, and that makes it all right, does it? You can just help yourself to anything you want as long as you bring it back? What would have happened if you had smashed it? Just tell me that.'

'He shouldn't have left the keys in it,' Kelly muttered defensively. 'If he didn't want anyone to touch it.'

Daphne was still making an effort to keep control of herself. 'So now it's *Paul's* fault,' she said tightly. 'Is that what you're saying? You can just help yourself? We have to keep everything nailed down?' She nodded towards the Robinson house. 'I was just phoning the police when you got back. A few seconds later and you would have been for the high jump.'

As Kelly's face fell, Helen Daniels stepped forward. 'There doesn't seem to be any harm done,' she said. 'I think we should let the matter drop.'

Jim Robinson's car turned into the driveway and pulled up behind Paul's. Daphne was still very angry. 'No, I'm sorry. I don't think I *can* let it drop.' She fixed Kelly with a relentless stare. 'I bailed you out. You promised to behave yourself.'

Kelly defiance was unfaltering. 'I didn't promise anything.'

'As far as I'm concerned,' Daphne snapped, 'bringing the car back does *not* make everything all right.'

Stepping out of his car, and carrying his squash racket, Jim Robinson began to walk admiringly around his son's new vehicle. 'Ah, so it's arrived,' he said.

Just arrived, Daphne thought wrily. 'I think we'll continue this discussion inside,' she said briskly to Kelly. She had a great deal more to say to the girl.

'Do you *really* want to go to gaol?' she demanded when they were back inside. When Kelly didn't answer she became caustic. 'Oh, I'm sorry, I forgot. You're so smart you wouldn't get caught, would you? Driving off in broad daylight in a brand new car that sticks out like a sore thumb.' Kelly still said nothing; her lack of response was causing Daphne to lose the impetus of her anger. 'You're not making this easy,' she said.

'You can still ring the cops,' Kelly said with a surly expression. 'It's not too late.'

'You're damned right it's not,' Daphne said forcefully. 'But the way you're going, it might be too late for you.' Oh, what was the use? She was just not getting through to the girl. She gestured in exasperation. 'It's like talking to a brick wall. It's bad enough that you have to steal at all,' she went on. 'But Paul Robinson is my neighbour. I have to face him every day.'

'Why do you think I brought it back?' Kelly asked quietly.

'Why did you?'

'A neat set of wheels like that.' Kelly smiled briefly. 'I could have been halfway up the coast by now. But I figured . . . you know . . . you helped me with my bail and everything. It wouldn't have been fair. So I brought it back – and now we're even.'

'We're even?'

Before she could query this further, Eileen came into the room. She glanced sourly at Kelly. 'Oh, you're still here,' she observed in a voice that was becoming stronger but was still far from normal.

'Yep.' Kelly nodded.

'Then I shall continue with my packing.'

'Eileen,' Daphne said as her mother-in-law turned away, 'there's no need for you to leave.'

Eileen sniffed. 'I think there is.'

Daphne sighed. 'Well, all right. If you insist. But you might as well have some lunch before you go. I've made a stew. It just needs to be heated up. I have to go out now to do some shopping, but I'm sure Kelly will help you.'

'Yeah.' Kelly didn't seem at all pleased by the prospect. 'Sure.'

'Daphne, I . . .'

But Daphne had had enough for one Saturday morning; she had her shopping to do.

Once again it was Paul's new car that forestalled her as she was leaving the house with her shopping basket. She heard a loud metallic thud; the sound of shattering glass; Paul's startled exclamation. Then she saw that his new car had rolled backwards down the driveway to crash into Jim Robinson's car which was parked just behind it.

Helen and Jim were running out of their house. Paul was staring in dismay at the damage to his car. 'Someone forgot to put the handbrake on,' Scott was saying as Daphne came up to them.

Paul rounded on him furiously. 'I did *not* forget to put the handbrake on,' he snarled. 'I never forget to put the handbrake on.'

'The way it rolled, when you patted it like that,' Scott pointed into the car. 'You can see it's not on.'

'It's not your fault, Paul,' Daphne told him dismally. She knew exactly who had left the handbrake off; she had hauled Kelly out of the car the moment she had pulled up in the driveway. Maybe there had been no time for Kelly to apply the handbrake; it was certainly the last thing that had been on Daphne's mind at the time.

'It was Kelly.' Lucy Robinson had just come running up to them. 'I saw her driving your car, Paul.'

'What?' Paul stared at her.

Jim Robinson placed his hand on his young daughter's shoulder. 'I think you'd better go inside now, Lucy,' he said. 'You, too, Scott.'

Lucy began to protest. 'But, Dad . . .'

Scott looked at his father with a puzzled frown. 'What's going on?'

'Come on,' Jim said more sharply. 'Move it!'

Shepherded by their father, they headed for the house with obvious reluctance. Paul stared angrily at Daphne. 'What's this about Kelly?' he demanded.

There was nothing for it but to come straight to the point. With a glance at Helen who had remained behind, possibly to offer her some moral support, Daphne said, 'She took your car for a drive.'

'She . . . *what*?'

'And she probably left the handbrake off.'

'That would explain everything, wouldn't it?' Paul angrily held up a piece of broken tail-light.

'It wasn't Daphne's fault,' Helen said.

'Thanks, Helen,' Daphne said as Paul glared at his grandmother. 'But, Paul, she is my responsibility. I'll pay for the damage.'

'Damn right you will,' Paul growled.

Helen was inspecting the rear of his car. 'Fortunately there doesn't appear to be much damage,' she observed.

'Look, Gran,' Paul said curtly. 'She could have wrapped it around a tree or something.'

'But she didn't, did she?'

'That's not the point.' His eyes narrowed suspiciously. 'You sound as if you're on her side.'

'I'm not on anybody's side,' Helen said levelly. 'I just don't see how taking it out on Daphne is going to solve anything.'

Paul considered this for a moment. 'You're right,' he said, abruptly turning on his heel and marching towards the Clarke house. 'Kelly's the one I should be taking it out on.'

'Paul, no.'

Helen began to follow Paul, but Daphne stopped her. 'Let him go, Helen.'

Helen looked worried. 'But he'll tear strips off her.'

Daphne smiled grimly. 'That might do her a world of good,' she said.

When Daphne returned to the house, she walked into another crisis. Eileen was making strange gargling sounds and clutching her throat while Kelly was watching her with a smile on her lips. 'What's going on?'

'Aaargh!' Eileen pointed accusingly at Kelly, then swallowed a glass of water. 'She tried to poison me.'

Whatever it was that had happened, it had at least had the effect of bringing her voice back to normal. 'It was just a bit of chilli,' Kelly told Daphne.

'A bit!' Eileen cried in anguish. 'My throat is on fire.' She swallowed some more water. 'She may have done irreparable damage.'

'I don't know.' Daphne wondered how much chilli Kelly *did* put in the stew. Knowing Kelly . . . 'At least your voice is back to normal.'

'Ah . . . yes.' Eileen sang a couple of scratchy notes, then frowned. 'It makes no difference. It was still a terrible thing to do.'

Daphne agreed with her. 'Yes, it was.'

Kelly defended herself. 'She was hassling me. After

Paul Robinson came in here and started throwing his weight around about that stupid car of his . . .'

'I warned you, Daphne,' Eileen broke in. 'I warned you about having this young thug under your roof. But did you listen to me? No, you didn't.' Her expression spoke eloquently of the crosses she had to bear in life. 'No one ever listens to me.'

'It's all right, Eileen,' Daphne said wearily.

But Eileen wasn't to be mollified. 'I can't remain in this house while . . .' she pointed dramatically at Kelly '. . . *she* is here. I mean, today it was the chilli. Tomorrow it could be rat poison.'

'Eileen, you're over-reacting.'

'I shall now finish my packing,' Eileen said importantly. 'Will you ask Desmond to bring my suitcases to the flat as soon as he returns.'

With her head held high and her bag clutched tightly under her arm, she sallied forth.

Kelly laughed softly. 'That was a good one,' she said. 'You know, the rat poison.' Daphne didn't think it was funny at all. Her expression remained stony. Kelly's smile faded. 'All right, I know what you're going to say. But she asked for it. Always on at me, nagging, nagging . . .'

'I'm not going to say anything, Kelly,' Daphne said sternly. 'You wouldn't listen to me, anyway. No,' she shook her head grimly, 'I think we've just got to face the fact that I made a mistake in bailing you out. A good stint in gaol is about the only thing that's going to make you wake up to yourself.'

'You want me to go then?'

Daphne relented a little. 'Have you had lunch?'

'What? With all that chilli?'

'It was a stupid thing to do,' Daphne said. 'Just as taking Paul's car like that was a stupid thing to do.'

She leaned closer to the girl. 'We are trying to help you – you must realise that.'

'So?' The old defiance was back. 'Did I ask for your help?'

'Yes, you did. Yesterday, in the bank.' Daphne laid her hand gently on the girl's shoulder. 'Look, Kelly, why don't you try opening up to people? They're not as bad as you think.'

'Really wonderful human beings.' Kelly pulled away from her. 'Just like my mum,' she said bitterly.

'So she kicked you out,' Daphne said. 'There are a lot of other people who haven't had it easy.'

'What would *you* know about that!' Kelly retorted. 'You've got it all in your lap. A nice house, your own business, married to the local bank manager. Oh yes, you really have it tough, don't you?'

Daphne's anger flared again. 'Sit down!' she commanded as Kelly made to leave the room. She pointed to the sofa. Kelly hesitated then, with an apprehensive expression, did as she was told. Her hands on her hips, Daphne towered over her. 'Don't tell *me* how easy I've got it,' she said in a clipped tone. 'Don't you *dare*. You don't know anything about me.' Her eyes bored steadily into the girl. 'Do you know what I was doing when I met Des? Do you?' Sitting nervously on the edge of the sofa, Kelly shook her head. 'I was a stripper. Yes, that's right,' she said when she saw the surprise register in the girl's eyes. 'I took my clothes off at bucks' parties. So,' she went on relentlessly, 'you're not the only one who's had to go it alone. Everything I've done, everything I've got, I've had to fight for – so don't tell *me* I don't know what it's like. I grew up with girls who make you look like a Sunday School teacher. Some of them had the guts to make a go of it, and the rest are either in gaol . . . or dead. That's the choice you're going to have to make, Kelly

– and you're going to have to make it pretty quickly. Because you're running out of time.'

Kelly slumped back in the sofa, all the fight knocked out of her by Daphne's outburst. 'I didn't mean . . .' Her voice trailed away. Daphne sat down beside her.

'So why don't you try? Give it a go?'

'We used to have terrible rows at home,' Kelly said distantly. 'My father always said I was to blame. I guess he was right. Then . . . then, one night I killed him.'

Daphne gave her a startled look. 'You what?'

'Oh, I didn't mean to,' Kelly said in that same small and distant voice. 'We were fighting over something stupid I had done. He was yelling and swearing at me. Then he started gasping and grabbing his chest. He died.'

'Oh, Kelly . . .'

'At the funeral, Mum just stared at me.' Kelly shook her head slowly; there were tears in her eyes. 'She blamed me for Dad's death. She hardly ever spoke to me after that. Even when I started getting into real trouble . . . shoplifting and stuff. If I tried to talk about it she would just turn away. I got into worse trouble. I told her I was leaving home and she just nodded. She was glad I was going. So that's what really happened. It was all my fault.' She sighed. 'I guess I always let down the people who try and help me.'

'The only person you're letting down is yourself.' Daphne was quite shaken by the girl's story.

'The last thing Dad yelled at me was that I was a no-hoper,' Kelly said bleakly. 'He was right, wasn't he?'

'No,' Daphne replied. 'He was wrong. And you're wrong to blame yourself for what happened.'

'I try to tell myself that,' Kelly said unhappily. 'I just keep seeing it happen. Over and over. Oh, Daph . . .' There was despair in her eyes as she turned to Daphne. 'What am I going to do?'

'What are *we* going to do,' Daphne corrected her as she took the girl's hand in her own.

Six

It was crude, it was barbaric, the way they were going about it. But if they really had to fight it out between themselves there was a better place to do it than in the street. 'I suggest we set up a proper boxing match,' Clive said. 'At the Police Boys' Club, a fortnight from today. Agreed?'

The two combatants shuffled their feet and avoided looking at each other. 'All right,' Mike Young said finally.

Clive turned to the other young warrior. 'Shane?'

'Ah . . . he'll keep till then, I guess,' Shane Ramsay muttered. 'That's if he keeps away from Jane.'

Ah yes, the young lady in question, the immediate source of the hostilities – Jane Harris, the pretty temptress who could provoke such passions in Ramsay Street. 'Let them fight,' she cried angrily to Clive Gibbons who had just stepped in to pull the fighting pair apart and thus create a very fragile peace in the street for the time being. 'Let them kill each other for all I care,' she said, striding away and leaving the three of them to stare after her with their mouths open.

The forthcoming battle was soon the talk of the street. Not everyone approved of it. 'I don't believe this,' Daphne Clarke exclaimed when she heard about it. 'Fighting over Jane as if she's a piece of property.'

Des Clarke winked at Mike. 'Faint heart never won fair maid,' he said. 'Hey, mate?'

'Des, don't encourage him,' Daphne said with a stern frown.

In the Ramsay household, Madge Mitchell was just as appalled. 'That sort of thing went out with the caveman, Shane,' she rebuked her nephew. 'Girls like to make up their own minds these days – and if I know Jane, fighting over her will be the quickest way of losing her.'

But Shane's confidence didn't falter for a moment. 'Don't worry, Auntie Madge. I'm not going to lose her. Not the fight, nor Jane.'

When Clive called at the Ramsay house that afternoon, Madge rounded on him. 'I'm ashamed of you, Clive Gibbons,' she challenged him the moment he put his head around the kitchen door.

'Me?' He looked startled.

'Yes, you. How can you, a doctor, encourage two young men to bash each other's brains out?'

'That's just what I'm trying to prevent,' Clive informed her in a reasonable tone.

'Oh yes?' Madge looked at him doubtfully.

'Look, Madge.' Clive advanced cautiously into the room. 'If I hadn't stepped in between them this afternoon one of them could have been seriously hurt.'

Madge was still unconvinced. 'And this way they won't?'

'The circumstances will be controlled. And it will be over in two rounds.'

'By a knockout,' Shane said, coming into the room with the new boxing gloves he had just picked up at a reduction sale.

'Oh . . . you idiots!' Madge turned away to continue her preparations for lunch.

It was Shane Clive had come to see. 'I'm running a check on the contestants' experience,' he said. 'Have you ever boxed before?'

'Not since I left school.'

Clive nodded as if this confirmed what he had already guessed. 'Then I am here to offer you my services as coach and manager.'

'You?' Shane's eyes widened in surprise.

'Yes. It so happens that my library contains one of the definitive books on the gentlemanly art of self-defence.' He had brought the book in question along with him. He presented it to Shane. 'You see? I can make you a champion in no time.'

Putting down his new boxing gloves, Shane leafed through the book. 'Yeah . . . well, I suppose I could do with a few tips.'

'Good. Training starts tonight.'

The next item on the agenda was to find a referee for the match. Clive thought he knew just the man for the job. 'What do you know about boxing?' he asked Jim Robinson.

Jim was surprised by the question. 'Well, I did go a few rounds at university,' he replied.

'Did you ever referee a match?'

'Police Boys' Club stuff. Paul did some boxing there a few years back. Why?'

'We seem to have a grudge match on our hands,' Clive told him. 'Mike and Shane have decided to put the gloves on to settle it – and what we need is an impartial referee. We would be honoured if you could do it.'

Jim considered the matter. 'All right,' he said at last. 'On one condition. That the fight is on the level.

And if I decide that someone looks like getting hurt, that's it, it's over, no arguments, no rematches.'

'Absolutely,' Clive said.

'I'll be in total control.'

'Of course.'

But it was really Clive's intention that the match shouldn't take place at all. He had a plan. 'Exercises, diets, forty-kilometre runs,' he told Jane, when she asked him to put a stop to the fight. 'And that's just the training. By the time I finish with Shane, he won't have the strength to fight a week-old kitten, let alone Mike.'

'Then Mike will have the advantage,' Jane pointed out to him.

'Des Clarke is training him.' Clive grinned at her. 'We've talked it over and decided that the more we try to make those two back off, the more aggressive they'll become. So . . . we encourage them to fight and then train them into exhaustion. They'll quit all by themselves.'

The light was beginning to dawn on Jane, the innocent cause of the bloodshed Clive was hoping to prevent. 'Sort of . . . reverse psychology?'

'You've got it, kid.' Clive was beaming proudly. 'Now am I brilliant, or what?'

Jane was smiling happily back at him. 'You're not only brilliant,' she said. 'You . . . you're fantastic.'

Clive lowered his head modestly. 'Yeah.'

The training was set to begin. Clive had a conference with Des Clarke. He showed him a book he had picked up called *Born to Win – The Psychology of Sports Motivation*. 'The theory is that no matter how fit you are, it's impossible for you to win if you've got the wrong attitude. That's the approach I intend to take with Shane.'

Des wasn't impressed. 'You're wasting your time,

mate,' he said. 'Mike is so fired up that he'll beat anyone.'

'Not Shane.'

'Including Shane. Mike is fighting for the honour of his true love.'

'So is Shane.'

Des frowned at him. 'Shane will be KO'd in the first round.' He suddenly remembered something. 'Well, that is if there's *going* to be a fight, which there isn't, that being what we've agreed.'

But Clive had been provoked by the reflection cast on his protégé. 'Mike couldn't fight a butterfly,' he said scornfully. 'He won't land a punch on Shane.'

'He will so.'

Clive drew back. 'There's no way to prove that, is there, as there's not going to be a fight.'

Des was becoming quite aggressive. 'If there *was* going to be a fight,' he snarled, 'then my boy would win. He's worth ten of yours.'

Clive glowered at him. 'Oh yeah? We'll see about that on the day. If there *was* going to be a day,' he added.

'Which there isn't.'

'Which there isn't,' Clive said crossly.

When Des was instructed by his bank's head office to attend a ten-day advance, training course in Albury, it seemed that here was an ideal excuse for the fight to be called off. 'No,' Mike protested violently when Des put this to him. 'No way.'

'But without me training you, Shane's going to have an unfair advantage.'

'I don't care. I'll train myself. There's no way I'm going to back down to Shane Ramsay.'

Des could see that he was fighting a losing battle. Mike just wouldn't be persuaded. 'Well, all right then,' he said with a resigned shrug. 'I'll have a word with Jim Robinson. Maybe he'll help with your training while I'm away.'

Mike nodded eagerly. 'That'd be good, Des.'

One more Des tried to make him see reason. 'Just do me a favour,' he said. 'Have a good long think about this fight. Suppose you *do* win . . . what would that prove, anyway? Jane won't want to have anything to do with you. Shane will probably never talk to you again. You'd probably end up losing more than you would gain.'

'I can't back down now, Des,' Mike said firmly.

This point having been reached, and with the training about to start in earnest, a spanner was thrown into the works by the sudden and unexpected arrival of Shane's grandfather, an old scrapper from way back who, having been told of the forthcoming fight in a letter from his daughter Madge, decided that his own talents in the field were definitely needed. 'With my experience and your ability,' he said, tossing back the brandy Shane had just poured for him, 'there's no way you'll lose this fight.'

Shane stared uneasily at his grandfather who had come all the way down from Queensland for the purpose of training him for the fight. 'But I've already got a trainer,' he protested.

'Who?'

'Clive.'

'That milksop!' Dan Ramsay snorted. 'He couldn't box his way out of a paper bag.' His wrinkled face creased even more as he smiled reassuringly at his youthful relative. 'I can see that I've arrived in the nick of time,' he said, reaching forward and patting Shane's knee. 'The family honour is at stake. You're a Ramsay, and you have to be trained by a Ramsay.' He tapped himself proudly on the chest. 'And I'm just the man for the job.'

'But, Granddad . . .'

The old man waved the protest aside. 'The first thing to do is sort out your training schedule.'

'I've already got one,' Shane said desperately. 'I get up at six, and train for an hour, then put in another hour after work.'

'You call that training?' Dan shook his head in reproach. 'From now on, you start at five. You put in a good three hours before work. And the same again in the evening.'

Shane stared at him in disbelief. 'Oh, come on . . .'

'If it was good enough for Jimmy Sharman's fighters,' Dan said flatly, 'it's good enough for you.'

'But times have changed, Granddad. It's over fifty years since you fought with the Jimmy Sharman troupe.'

'I'm as fit as a mallee bull.' Dan thumped himself on the chest. 'Always have been.' He shook his head sorrowfully as he surveyed the grandson who was about to defend the honour of the Ramsay name. 'You've had it too soft, Shane. When I've finished with you, you won't know what has hit you.'

'Terrific,' Shane groaned. 'Oh, that's just terrific.'

The fact that Shane's training schedule was about to be taken over by his grandfather was a severe blow to Clive's plans. 'You can't do it,' he cried as he confronted the old man.

'What's the matter, Gibbons?' Dan regarded him leerily. 'Scared I'll show you up?' His seamed face hardened. 'You've done a sloppy job on my grandson, that's for sure. He's in no better condition than a . . . a . . .' He sought for the appropriate word '. . . a marshmallow.'

'Yes, but you don't understand . . .'

'Oh, I understand all right,' Dan said gruffly. 'The

Ramsay honour is at stake, and I'm here to do something about it.'

'But there doesn't *have* to be any fight.'

Dan looked at him in disgust. 'I suppose you're hoping they'll just kiss and make up.'

'Something along those lines,' Clive muttered.

As Shane entered the room, his grandfather bore down on him. 'What about it?' he demanded. 'Are you going through with it or not?'

Shane wasn't so sure now; Jane had just given him an ultimatum. 'I'm starting to wonder.'

Clive relaxed slightly at this hopeful development. Dan Ramsay, on the other hand, was aghast. 'You can't chicken out now.'

'But what will it prove?' Shane asked.

'I'll tell you what it will prove.' He prodded Shane's chest with his forefinger as he spoke. 'It'll prove that the Ramsays are not a pack of weak Cyrils that'll let the rest of the world stomp all over them.' He stopped prodding Shane. 'You've got to go through with this fight, Shane, my boy. For the sake of the Ramsays.'

Shane was wavering again. Clive stepped into the discussion. 'Aren't you being a bit melodramatic about this?' he asked Dan.

'You keep out of this,' Dan snapped, then turned back to his grandson. 'If you back out of this now, you'll regret it for the rest of your life.'

Shane frowned thoughtfully. 'Maybe you're right.'

'Now you're talking.' Dan clapped him warmly on the shoulder.

Seeing that Shane had been won over again after his brief moment of uncertainty, Clive nevertheless still tried to make him see reason. 'It won't do you any good with Jane,' he said.

'I know,' Shane said with a shrug. 'But it will make

me feel a hell of a lot better.' He nodded at Dan. 'The fight's still on.'

Dan chuckled. 'I'll make sure you kill the other bloke,' he said happily.

Clive was dismayed by this turn of events; it was the very last thing he had wanted to happen.

For Madge Mitchell, too, her father's arrival was extremely unwelcome. 'What are you doing here?' she demanded sourly on her return from work.

'Don't be like that, Madge. Someone had to come and save the family honour.'

'What?'

'Young Shane's boxing match. I've come to give him the benefit of my great experience.'

'Oh, you have, have you?' Madge said shortly. 'Well, you can turn around and go right back to Queensland. This whole fight business has gone far enough. I don't want you encouraging Shane.'

Shane himself arrived home from work. 'Oh, there you are,' Dan greeted him. 'Right now, track suit on, thirty push-ups, then five miles around the block, and then . . .'

'Oh, hang on, Granddad,' Shane groaned as he slumped down on a chair. 'I've only just finished work. I'm beat. And, anyway, I said we'd *talk* about my training.'

Dan gave a snort of contempt. 'No use talking about it. You'll never get fit that way.'

'Oh, stop it, Dad.' Madge frowned down at Shane. 'You're not really going through with this ridiculous fight, are you?'

'Too right I am,' Shane replied seriously. 'And if Granddad can help me win it . . .' He pushed himself up from the chair. 'Maybe a quick jog around the block won't hurt after all,' he said to Dan. 'I'll just go and change.'

'That's the spirit.' Dan began to perform some nifty boxing manoeuvres; his fists flailed the air. 'We'll show the world that us Ramsays are not to be messed around with. I'll have you so fit,' he promised his grandson, 'that Mike will be counted out in the first round.'

The training was begun in earnest. There were push-ups and sit-ups, long runs and prolonged skipping bouts. Down at the Police Boys' Club, the punching bag was pummelled ferociously. 'What are we going to do?' Clive Gibbons asked with an expression of gloom. 'We can't let them get into the ring together. They'll murder each other.'

'Well, since you're no longer Shane's coach,' Jim Robinson said, 'I hereby nominate you as referee. That way, if anyone looks like being hurt you can stop the fight.'

'I don't want either of them to get hurt.'

'How are you going to stop it?' Jim queried. 'If they don't do it that way, they'll end up scrapping here in Ramsay Street.'

'Yeah, I suppose you're right,' Clive said with a sigh.

In the Ramsay house, Dan was demonstrating to Shane some of the finer points in the art of boxing. 'A matter of footwork,' he was saying. 'Footwork and balance. When you throw a punch, you should have all your weight behind it. And if your balance isn't right . . . over you go.'

Madge came into the room with some flowers she had just arranged in a vase. 'Oh, listen to Muhammad Ali Ramsay, will you,' she said drily.

'Float like a butterfly and sting like a bee.' Shane waltzed around the room and made feinting jabs in the air; his footwork was quick.

'I know what I'm talking about,' Dan said shortly.

'Me and Jimmy Sharman were just like that.' He held up a pair of crossed fingers.

'Oh yes.' Madge placed the flowers on the table. 'Keeping your fingers crossed so you wouldn't be knocked out.'

'There's never been a Ramsay carried out of the ring,' Dan boasted.

'There's always a first time.'

While the training went on, attempts were still made to persuade the rivals for Jane's affection to call off the fight. 'Oh no, not you too,' Shane said uncomfortably when Daphne Clarke approached him for that purpose.

'Six weeks ago, you and Mike were the best of friends,' Daphne said. 'And now . . .'

'What's this?' Dan Ramsay broke in. 'Has Mike got a *woman* fighting his battles now?'

'I'm not fighting anyone's battles.' Daphne looked at him severely. 'I'm trying to stop one.'

'Is Mike scared of getting hurt then?'

'Mike can look after himself.'

'So let him prove it,' Dan said testily. 'In the ring, like a man.'

'Yes, a man with no brains,' Madge chipped in. 'Like a couple of other people I could mention.'

Dan glowered at her. 'You keep out of this, Maggie.'

'And don't call me Maggie.'

Voices began to be raised. 'If Mike wants to fight,' Shane cried, 'I'll be there.'

Dan was bearing down on Daphne. 'You tell Mike to stop hiding behind a woman's skirt,' he growled.

Daphne stood her ground. 'I just don't want to see anyone get hurt.'

'Oh, stop it!' Madge said sharply. 'All of you.'

They stopped their aguing for a moment to look at

her. Then Dan turned back to Daphne. 'Shane will be in the ring on the night,' he promised her with a slow and not very pleasant smile. 'If Mike doesn't turn up, we'll understand.'

'Oh, to hell with you.' Daphne had lost her patience altogether. 'I came here to try and talk some sense into you. But you lot . . .' she glared at Shane and his grandfather '. . . you wouldn't know common sense if you tripped over it.' At the door, she stopped and turned back into the room. 'Mike *will* be fighting Shane,' she assured them with vehemence. 'And I'll be cheering him on. Because as far as I'm concerned, if he's fighting the Ramsays he's taking on the village idiots.' She slammed the door behind her.

Madge was stricken by this parting shot of Daphne's. She rounded on her father. 'Well, are you satisfied now?' she demanded furiously. 'Not only have you put Shane in a position where he's likely to get hurt, but you—' she waved her finger in front of his nose '—you've started a feud with the neighbours as well.'

Dan stared blandly back at her. 'I didn't start anything.'

'Oh, you—' Words suddenly failing her, Madge stormed out of the room.

'Now like I was saying . . .' With a shrug, Dan turned back to Shane. 'When you throw a punch, you've got to keep your arm straight—'

While Des was away, Daphne decided to take Mike's training in her own hands. Who did those Ramsays think they were, anyway? Just because the street was named after some distant relative, that didn't mean they could run the whole neighbourhood. 'You're going to show them, Mike,' she told her new protégé. 'And I'm going to make sure you do. We'll put you on a protein diet, jogging, work-outs in the gym . . .'

'But Jim's my trainer,' Mike reminded her. 'Remember?'

'Oh yes.' Daphne had quite forgotten. 'Yes, he can help of course. But I'm sure his heart is not in it. Mine is. At least right now it is.'

The whole neighbourhood seemed to be taking sides on the matter. 'I'd rather this family kept out of it,' Helen Daniels said.

'That's a little difficult,' Paul Robinson pointed out to her, 'when you consider that Dad is Mike's trainer.'

'There's no way Dan is going to let it die,' Jim remarked. 'He's having a ball, turning this into a feud between the Ramsays and the Robinsons.'

'Well, at the risk of sounding disloyal,' Paul said, 'I really don't think Mike has much of a chance.'

Jim Robinson frowned thoughtfully. 'Oh, I don't know,' he murmured. 'He's young, he's fit. He's probably faster than Shane.'

Helen Daniels wasn't finding this subject at all pleasant. 'Could we drop this, please?'

'Sorry, Gran,' Paul said, then looked at his father. 'All the same, I wouldn't pin my hopes on Mike if I were you.'

Jim was beginning to get annoyed. 'What would you know about boxing?' he queried.

'More to the point.' Paul regarded him levelly. 'What would *you* know? I mean, you're training Mike . . .'

'Are you saying I don't know what I'm doing?' Jim demanded with some belligerence.

'Jim!'

'No, it's all right, Helen,' Jim said to his mother-in-law, who was looking decidedly unhappy. 'I just want to know if my son has any faith in me, or not.'

'It's not a question of faith, Dad,' Paul said. 'It's just facing the facts. I mean, you don't know as much about boxing as Dan does.'

'Do you want to bet?'

'Ten dollars says that Shane will win.'

'Ten dollars? Is that all? I have more faith in Mike than that. Make it a hundred.'

'Jim, really!' Helen said in disgust.

But father and son paid no attention to her as they faced each other challengingly across the kitchen table. 'All right,' Paul said. 'If you *really* want to make it worthwhile, why not five hundred?'

'This is quite ridiculous,' Helen exclaimed.

Paul glanced at her. 'Gran, I'm just making a point.'

'And you've made it,' Jim said forcefully. 'You're on. Five hundred it is then.'

'Done.' Paul's smile was confident as they shook hands on the deal.

The feud was gradually gathering impetus. Dan Ramsay began to needle Jim Robinson. 'Thought you might be doing some training yourself,' he said with a smirk as he executed a slow overarm toss. 'To throw in the towel.'

Jim was hosing down his car as Dan called to him from next door. He was sorely tempted to point the hose where it would do the most good. 'I can see where your sons get it from,' he said curtly. 'All talk and no action, too.'

Now it was Dan's turn to become hot under the collar. 'Oh, you want action, son, do you? Then you'd better take out some insurance. I can handle myself. I used to be a flamin' contender.'

'Max told me you used to box,' Jim said deliberately. 'What did they call you? Canvas-back Ramsay?'

Dan bristled. 'I never had any trouble handling the Robinsons, sonny,' he retorted. 'The only one with a decent left hook in your family was your grandmother. The Robinsons were always easy meat.'

Jim had taken enough of this. He advanced threateningly on his tormentor. 'And *your* family likes making trouble,' he shouted as Dan warily backed away from him. 'They like it for breakfast, lunch and dinner.' He was very angry. 'Your thick-headed grandson thinks he can solve his problems with his fists. And now you want to turn it into World War Three.'

'You leave him alone, Jim Robinson!' Madge Mitchell was hurrying towards them from the house next door. 'Picking on a defenceless old man.'

With a quick glance at her, Dan winced and placed his hand on his chest. 'I felt a twinge, Maggie . . .'

Madge gave Jim a fierce look. 'You should be ashamed of yourself,' she said angrily.

There were more people converging on the scene. Mike Young had emerged from the Clarke house; Clive Gibbons had just arrived to see what the fuss was about. Seeing them, Dan Ramsay pointed accusingly at Jim. 'Go on!' he yelled. 'Go on! Bring all your mates. Three to one. Typical Robinson trick.'

Clive was trying to defuse the situation. 'Come on, Dan,' he urged. 'Be reasonable.'

'Mind your own business.'

'Dad, please calm yourself.' Madge's face was taut with fury as she faced Jim again. 'I'm going to see Helen about this,' she said, moving up the driveway to the Robinson house.

Clive was still trying to make himself heard. 'Dan, please. You do realise, don't you, that this street is a credit to the family name?' Dan gaped at him; Clive pressed his advantage. 'We all manage to get on with one another, most of the time,' he continued. 'And that's a small miracle in this day and age. And just to make sure we keep it that way, I suggest we all get together and talk it through.' He gave Dan and Jim a warm and encouraging smile. 'How about it?'

Jim shrugged. 'Fine by me.'

Dan frowned uncertainly. 'Don't see what there is to talk about,' he muttered. 'Still . . .'

'So if we step into Jim's place,' Clive suggested.

'Not on your life.' Dan shook his head emphatically. 'If you want to talk, we'll talk on Ramsay property.'

Clive looked inquiringly at Jim. Jim nodded. 'All right,' he said.

Meanwhile, in the Robinson house, Helen Daniels and Madge Mitchell had come to an agreement to put an end to this nonsense right there and then. 'Will you speak to Jim then?' Madge asked.

Helen frowned slightly as she thought about it. 'Well . . . apart from this ridiculous bet he's having with Paul,' she said slowly, 'I think he's been fairly reasonable.'

Madge's expression tightened. 'You should have heard the way he was abusing Dad just now.'

For Helen there was another way of looking at that. 'Madge, you must admit that your father is the one who has been stirring up all this. I must say,' she added for good measure, 'that the men in your family certainly like to throw their weight around.'

This was too much for Madge. Her face reddened. 'I will *not* listen to you saying things against my family,' she said, her voice rising in outrage.

'Be reasonable, Madge,' Helen said evenly. 'You know what the Ramsays are like. Your brothers Max and Tom. Your father – I think he's even worse.'

Madge leapt loyally to the defence of her family. 'While we're on the subject of families,' she said in a low, vibrant voice. 'I wouldn't be throwing stones if I were you.'

'What is that supposed to mean?' Helen demanded.

'Just that the Ramsays aren't the only family with problems around here,' Madge returned angrily as she made for the door.

She stormed back to her own house. 'If the Robinsons want war,' she cried, 'then they've got it.'

Everyone stared at her. 'What happened?' Shane asked.

'What happened? I've just been stabbed in the back by my so-called friend, that's what happened.' She caught sight of Jim Robinson. 'What is *he* doing in my house?'

Clive Gibbons was making placating gestures. 'Madge, please. It's a peace conference.'

'Right,' Madge snorted. 'I'll give you five minutes.' Turning on her heel, she stomped out of the room.

'Forget it, Clive,' Jim said heavily. 'There's no point.'

'I called a peace conference,' Clive insisted. 'And I'm going to have a peace conference, even if I have to—' He took a deep breath, and looked around the room. 'All right, it's confession time,' he said. 'The boxing match was my idea. I never actually intended it to take place.' He glanced first at Shane then at Mike, who were sitting stiffly at opposite ends of the room. 'We figured that the rigorous training would knock some of the aggro out of you two. And because you are both intelligent, sensible guys, we thought that you would realise that violence solves nothing. Now, unless you want to put evolution back a couple of million years, don't you think that's true?'

He could see by their expressions of uncertainty that they had been swayed by his argument. Dan Ramsay, on the other hand, was disgusted by it. 'Kiss and make up, eh?' he rasped. 'You bunch of girl guides.' He turned to Shane. 'Typical Robinson stunt. They're pulling a swifty . . .' he gestured brusquely towards Mike '. . . to give that runt a chance to save his skin.'

Mike leapt to his feet. 'That's a lie!'

'Are you calling my granddad a liar?' Shane was also on his feet.

'You bet I am.'

'All right, mate.' Shane stood with his arms out from his sides, his head thrust forward belligerently. 'Forget the training, forget everything. Let's have it out now.'

Mike returned his opponent's hostile stare. 'That suits me just fine,' he said.

Clive slumped back in his chair. So much for the peace conference, he thought miserably.

The gym was booked for lunch-time that day. 'This isn't necessary,' Clive said to Shane after Jim and Mike had gone.

'It's a question of honour, Clive,' Shane said calmly.

Madge came back into the room. When she saw that Jim Robinson had gone she gave a satisfied nod. 'The blue's on for lunch-time,' Dan told her with relish.

Madge raised her eyebrows. 'Today?'

Clive hadn't given up in his attempts to stop the fight. 'You're all getting worked up over nothing.' He appealed once more to Shane. 'Do you honestly think you can win a girl like this?' he asked, then shook his head. 'It's caveman stuff, mate. Now . . .' he smiled encouragingly. 'Why don't you shake hands with Mike. Let Jane decide who she wants to be with.'

'Peace with honour,' Dan Ramsay sneered. 'That's what Neville Chamberlain said just before Hilter punched him up the throat.' He gestured contemptuously at Clive. 'If he's the referee,' he said to Shane, 'I don't like it.'

'It will be a fair fight,' Clive protested.

A short while later, Jane came to the Ramsay house to add her pleas for restraint. She began by being caustic. 'I just came over to thank you for calling off the fight,' she said.

'I only said I would think about it,' Shane muttered awkwardly.

He was lying face down on the kitchen table while his grandfather, with only a few hours to get him into shape, massaged him.

'Now, now,' Dan chided Jane. 'None of this soppy stuff. The boy musn't be distracted.'

Jane ignored him. 'I'm asking you again, Shane. Call the whole thing off.'

'I can't. It's too late.'

Dan continued to pummel his grandson's body. Jane said angrily, 'Having two guys smash each other about over them might appeal to some girls, but it doesn't appeal to me. I meant what I said before, Shane. If you go through with this, I never want to see you again.'

Shane looked unhappy. 'No Ramsay ever walked away from a stoush,' Dan said importantly, pausing in his manipulations. 'The whole street would laugh at him.' His eyebrows knit into a formidable frown. 'And I won't have any grandson of mine being called a coward by that Robinson mob.'

'It's not just you and me any more, Jane,' Shane said sadly. 'It's more than that.'

'Well, you won't be able to make *me* the excuse for it any more,' Jane cried, crossing to the door. 'And nor will Mike.'

He was doing really well for himself, Shane thought

dejectedly. He had lost his girl, and most of his friends – and the fight hadn't even started yet.

The fight was almost due to start. Daphne glared balefully at Clive, who she had found in a far corner of the gym, pedalling an exercise bike as he studied his book of boxing rules. 'If there's one mark on that boy . . .'

'Don't worry, Daphne. I'm going to stop this the first chance I get.'

In the dressing room, Daphne had already issued her last-minute instructions to Mike while Jim Robinson fitted on his boxing gloves. Keep your head down, she had told him, and your hands up; let your opponent come on strong, then push him back with his left. 'How do you propose we do that?' she asked Clive.

'Don't know yet.' Clive frowned worriedly at the rule book. 'This isn't much help. It keeps referring to physical damage . . .'

Dan Ramsay was also giving some last-minute advice. 'Pain, boy,' he was saying. 'You've got to learn to love pain.'

'Don't talk so much rubbish, Dad,' Madge said in exasperation. 'We don't want him hurt.'

'You keep out of this,' Dan said sternly. 'A Ramsay can take punishment. You let him pour it on, Shane,' he advised his grandson, 'and then you can take him apart.'

All the Robinsons and the Ramsays had turned up at the Police Boys' Club for the match. Daphne and Des were there. Even Jane Harris, the innocent cause of it all, had turned up. The rival supporters were ranged on opposite sides of the ring. As the combatants climbed into the ring, there was a great deal of shouted encouragement, which soon degenerated into a volley of insults exchanged from one side to the other. Deciding he had better take charge before he had an all-out brawl on his hands, Clive called for silence. He had to do it a few times before he was finally heeded. He thought he might ease matters if he began the proceedings with a joke.

'No doubt you're all wondering why I called you here today . . .' There was no response; everyone was looking at him blankly. He smiled ruefully. 'Oh well, I suppose a sense of humour is too much to expect.' He became serious. 'Looking around me, I see a lot of aggression in people who were once . . . good neighbours . . .'

'Get on with it!' Dan roared.

Clive shrugged, and from his position in the centre of the ring signalled the contestants to join him. The three of them huddled closely together, Clive in the middle as he consulted his rule book. 'Each round goes for two minutes,' he told the two tense warriors. 'There's no kicking, gouging or hitting below the belt. And when I call break, you break.'

Both eager to get in with the first blow, Mike and Shane were straining like two racehorses at the starting gate. 'Just keep out of the way, Mike,' Jim called.

'Go at him from the jump,' Dan instructed Shane.

'Each round starts when the bell goes,' Clive said, with a glance at Susan Cole whom he had nominated as time keeper because her role in the affair was a neutral one. 'Okay, Susan?'

Obligingly, Susan rang the bell. 'Hang on, not yet,' Clive yelped as, at the sound of the bell, Mike and Shane swung at the same time. There were two sickening thuds as the blows connected, then a gasp as Clive, who had been sandwiched between them, sank slowly to the canvas and lay still.

There was a stunned silence, then someone called, 'Get a doctor.'

'He is a doctor,' someone else said.

Clive was out for no more than a minute or two. Sitting up, he gingerly felt his jaw. 'It's okay,' he announced a little shakily. 'No bones broken.' He blinked up at Shane and Mike who were staring down at him with uncertainty in their eyes. 'Who won?'

'It hasn't started yet,' Jim told him.

Clearly, the fight had been taken out of both boys. 'What are you waiting for?' Clive demanded.

'Yeah.' Dan Ramsay was impatient for the fight to get underway. 'Go on, get on with it.'

Shane and Mike gave each other a quick, unsure glance. Jane came up to the side of the ring. 'Couldn't we end this now?' she implored. 'Please . . .'

'Yeah.' Mike looked hesitantly at Shane. 'Clive could have been hurt pretty badly,' he said. 'I'll call it off if you will.'

Dan Ramsay groaned in dismay. 'You're not letting him off the hook, are you?'

'Stay out of it, Granddad.' Shane gave him a sharp look. 'Like Mike said, it could have been a nasty accident.'

As he and Mike touched gloves, there was a round of applause. Clive beamed in profound satisfaction. All was well that ended well, even if his jaw could have been broken in the process. 'All bets are off, I suppose,' Paul Robinson said to his father.

Jim nodded. 'Looks that way to me.'

Madge came up to Helen. 'I do feel rather foolish,' she said in embarrassment.

'No more than the rest of us,' Helen happily assured her.

And so peace was restored to the street. In less than a month is would be Christmas.

Seven

There was something fishy about this clergyman; something not quite right. Paul had the first inkling of this when he remembered that the chaplain he had met at the Lincoln Detention Centre on the night Terry died had been a much older man.

'Ah, yes. . . .' Paul noted the momentary hesitation at his mention of this. 'That was my relief. I wasn't on duty at the time.' The Reverend Errol Price gave a mournful sigh. 'I wasn't there when Terry needed me most.'

He had been there when Paul arrived home that evening. When his father had introduced him and told him that he had come to talk about Terry, Paul had refused to listen; the memories were still too close, too bitter. Terry was dead, and Paul was the one who had to live with it. They all had to live with it, the minister had replied. Jim Robinson had persuaded his son to give the man a hearing at least.

'It wouldn't have made much difference,' Paul said shortly. 'I mean, there was nothing you could have done. It's just the way Terry was.'

'All the same . . .' A distant look came into Errol Price's eyes. 'Just . . . something.'

They were on edge enough as it was. Helen wasn't

home; she hadn't been home all day, and no one knew where she was. It was strange that she should have gone out without letting anyone know where she was. They were beginning to worry about her.

Because Helen wasn't there to cook their evening meal, it had been decided to send Scott out for pizzas rather than bother preparing something for themselves. Now Scott arrived back with the food. When he saw the Reverend Errol Price, he stopped short and looked at him with a puzzled expression. 'This is my other son,' Jim Robinson told the man of the cloth. 'Scott, this is Reverend Price. He knew Terry.'

Paul saw that Price was looking a little ill at ease. 'Didn't I see you in the street this morning?'

'Yes . . . yes.' The clergyman turned to Jim. 'I intended calling on your earlier,' he explained. 'But, unfortunately, I found I had left my address book at home. I wasn't sure exactly which house it was.' He rose to his feet. 'Now I'll leave you with your dinner,' he said with a smile. 'I'm very glad to have met you all.'

Jim showed him to the door. 'Perhaps you'd like to come back tomorrow,' he suggested. 'I'm sure Helen would like to meet you.'

'Yes,' Price said. 'I'm sorry I missed her.'

Jim came back into the living room with a rebuke for his older son. 'You might at least have tried to be polite,' he said gruffly.

'Dad, don't start,' Paul muttered resentfully. 'I don't want anyone bringing up my past again – minister or no minister. It's not my fault that he's losing sleep because he wasn't there the night Terry died.'

Jim regarded his son coolly. 'Maybe it hasn't occurred to you that he came here because he thought *you* might be losing sleep, too,' he said.

'I thought I was coping very well,' Paul said unhappily. 'Until he showed up.'

'Were you, Paul?' Jim queried shrewdly. 'Sometimes I wonder.'

And if the truth be known, Paul sometimes wondered, too. Terry . . . She had asked to see him, but he had refused. Then she had taken the pills. She hadn't regained consciousness. 'Just leave it, Dad,' he muttered. 'Please.'

There was still no sign of Helen. Jim snapped at Scott to get off the telephone. He didn't want it tied up in case Helen was trying to reach them. 'She's probably just with some friends,' Paul suggested. 'She's lost track of time, that's all.' All the same, it was getting late.

Little Lucy picked up on this point. 'Gran *never* comes home late,' she insisted. 'Not without telling us where she is first.'

They all had to accept the reality of this. 'Maybe I should call some of her friends,' Paul said.

Jim nodded. 'All right.'

'I'll use the office phone so this one isn't tied up. I'll check her diary. There might be something in that.'

'Good idea.' Jim followed him to the door. He lowered his voice so that the others wouldn't hear. 'If you don't have any luck there, try the hospitals, just in case.'

But the response was negative all round. None of her friends who Paul managed to contact had seen Helen or heard from her that day. With the hospitals, too, he drew a blank. He did make one interesting discovery, however. 'I've found her car,' he told his father when he returned to the house early the following morning.

'Where?' Jim was instantly wide awake.

'It was in the car park at work. I didn't see it there last night.'

'Then someone put it there.'

'I said I didn't see it there,' Paul pointed out to him. 'That doesn't necessarily mean it wasn't there.'

'Yeah.' Jim had been up all night; his clothes were rumpled; he was unshaven and looked very tired. 'I've called the police.'

'What did they say?'

'Well, as a matter of fact they weren't very interested.'

'Your kidding.' Scott had just come into the room.

'Your grandmother is past the age of consent,' Jim wearily reminded him. 'She's quite entitled to stay out all night if she wants to. They even suggested that she might have wanted a night out on her own.'

Scott said bleakly, 'But Gran wouldn't go off without telling us.'

'*I* know that,' Jim said heavily, 'and *you* know that. But you have to look at it from their point of view. They receive dozens of calls like this every day. Ninety-five percent of them turn out to be false alarms.'

'Oh yes?' Paul was also staring at his father. 'And what about the other five percent?'

Leaving his father beside the telephone, Paul decided to check the neighbours. At Clive Gibbons' house, he ran into Mrs Mangel.

'Oh, Mister Robinson,' she greeted him in a voice of concern. 'Is there any news of Mrs Daniels?'

'No, not yet,' Paul replied with a shake of his head. 'In fact, I'm just checking to see if anyone did see her yesterday.' He eyed them intently. 'Are you absolutely positive that neither of you saw her?'

'No.' Clive shook his head. 'Sorry.'

Mrs Mangel was frowning thoughtfully. 'I've just

thought. There must have been *someone* home when that minister came round, because someone let him in.'

'Last night?' Paul was puzzled. 'But Dad was there. And Lucy.'

'No, no,' Mrs Mangel said quickly. 'Before lunch. Oh . . . eleven-thirty at the latest. I remember because I was vacuuming my front room. And I thought how strange it was that a minister should be calling.'

'Mrs Mangel, thank you very much,' Paul cried in excitement as he began to run back to the house. 'Thanks a lot. You're a marvel.'

Jim looked up at him in surprise as he hurried into the living room. 'I thought you said that the Reverend Price hadn't met Gran,' Paul said breathlessly.

'That's right.' Jim's forehead was creased in a puzzled frown.

'Then what was he doing here yesterday morning?'

'Eh?' Jim looked startled.

'Mrs Mangel said she saw him about eleven o'clock,' Paul explained. 'And Gran let him in. It's strange, isn't it, that he didn't mention it.'

'It could be an oversight,' Jim suggested cautiously.

'Oh, come off it, Dad.' There was no way that Paul could see it as an oversight; he'd had his doubts about that clergyman from the beginning. 'He actually said he was sorry to have missed her.'

Jim was still uncertain. 'Let's not make any wild accusations till we've got some proof.'

'Fine,' Paul said tersely. 'That's fine by me.' If his father wanted proof, Paul knew just where to obtain it.

Scott was out. A despondent Lucy had been persuaded to take the dog for a walk. Paul made a telephone call. 'I've just been on to the gaol,' he told his father when he had finished. 'And yes, there is a chaplain called Price. But he's on holiday at the moment.'

'Then that explains how he had time to come here,' Jim remarked with a shrug.

Now, with a gleam of triumph in his eyes, Paul delivered his bombshell. 'Dad, Reverend Price – the real Reverend Price – is fifty-two years old.'

The Reverend Price who had come to the house had been nowhere near that age; he had been a young man with dark hair and wide, staring eyes. 'Oh, my God,' Jim breathed when Paul's revelation had sunk in.

'I *said* there was another chaplain at the gaol on the night Terry died,' Paul went on. 'And there's only the one chaplain at the gaol.' He shook his head emphatically. 'The guy who was here last night was definitely not him.'

'Then who is he? What is he up to?'

'I've no idea. But I know one thing for sure. He has to have something to do with Gran's disappearance.'

'Then we've got to find him,' Jim said urgently.

'Sure. But how?'

'He said he would be back today.'

'Maybe.' Paul thoughtfully scratched his chin. 'But if he doesn't come back, where do we start looking?'

They were still pondering the matter when Lucy and the dog returned from their walk. Peremptorily over-riding her protests, Jim sent her to her room; he and Paul had things to discuss. 'I don't think we should call the police about this fellow yet,' he said after Lucy had left the room, 'that's all.'

'Well, I still say we should do something,' Paul protested.

'And if we're on the wrong horse?'

'You think we'll look like idiots,' Paul retorted. 'Is that it?'

'No . . .'

Paul was working hard to convince his father. 'Look, Dad, I don't know what sort of stunt this Reverend Price, or whoever the hell he is, is trying to pull. But I'll bet you anything you like that he has something to do with Gran's disappearance.'

But Jim Robinson was not a man who liked taking chances. 'I'd like more evidence first,' he said quietly.

'What more evidence do you *need*, for heaven's sake?' Paul was becoming exasperated by his father's stubbornness. 'Look, you *know* he's not who he says he is. And the guy I spoke to at the prison didn't make any mistake. The real Reverend Price is the one I saw at the prison hospital that night – I'm sure of it. Look, Dad, be reasonable,' he pleaded, when he saw that Jim was still not altogether moved by his argument. 'Gran has disappeared. This guy turns up. It *can't* be a coincidence. I say he's *got* to have something to do with it.'

Just then, before Jim had time to raise any more objections, Lucy came running into the room. 'Dad!'

Jim frowned at her in annoyance. 'I thought I told you to stay in your room.'

'But the Reverend is coming up the driveway. I saw him from my window.'

This news made the matter even more urgent. 'I'll *make* him tell us where Gran is,' Paul muttered threateningly. 'Even if I have to beat it out of him.'

'No, Paul, that's not going to work.'

'Then what do you suggest?' The doorbell would be ringing at any moment now; Paul was becoming frantic.

Jim was thinking hard. 'Well, he might be the only person who knows where Helen is,' he said. 'We've got to play along with him, so that he doesn't suspect that we know anything. Hopefully he'll let something slip.'

Lucy was staring at them in wide-eyed wonder as she tried to fathom what all this was about. 'All right,' Paul said grudgingly. 'We'll do it your way. But if anything goes wrong, I'm going to take things into my own hands.'

His face clearing, Jim turned to his daughter. 'Lucy, darling, I want you to go over to the Ramsays.'

'But, Dad . . .'

'Off you go. This is serious.' He pushed her gently towards the door. 'Out the back door.'

The doorbell sounded. Jim answered it. 'Good morning, Mister Robinson.' The Reverend Errol Price greeted him with a smile.

'Reverend Price. Good morning.'

'I trust Mrs Daniels arrived home safe and sound.'

'No, she didn't. We don't know where she is.'

'Oh dear.' Errol Price's expression mirrored his concern. 'I know how difficult this must be for you all. If you will allow me to share the burden . . .'

'That's very thoughtful of you.' Jim moved to one side. 'We were hoping you might call by. Please come in.'

'Yes, I can understand how distressing this must be for you,' Errol Price said sympathetically when he was seated in the living room. 'I myself have lost someone close to me.' He looked across at Paul who was making a very real effort to curb his impatience. 'And it must be doubly hard on you. So soon after Terry's death.' His pale eyes were wide and intense as he stared at Paul who had just stiffened at the mention of his former wife's name. 'You must feel some responsibility for that . . . in the circumstances.'

Maybe. But she was in gaol because she had tried

to kill him after he had found out about her involvement in Charles Durham's murder and was on the point of calling the police. Responsibility? She had asked to see him, but he had refused. 'Well, that's just something I've learned to live with,' he muttered.

Perhaps alerted by the coldness of Paul's tone, the clergyman was studying him closely. 'Yes. I suppose acceptance of God's will *is* the wisest choice.'

Jim offered to make tea. Errol Price looked uncertainly at Paul. He seemed to be suddenly on edge. 'Forgive me if I upset you by mentioning Terry,' he said. 'Perhaps . . . if you confront your grief, bring it all out into the open . . . ?' He smiled wanly. 'I'll be only too willing to lend an ear.'

'Paul,' Jim called from the kitchen. 'Do you know where that spare jug element is?'

Relieved and grateful for the opportunity to talk to his father alone, Paul hurried into the kitchen. 'Be careful,' Jim warned him in a whisper. 'Just take it easy. He's getting rattled by your attitude.'

'I still say we make him tell us,' Paul whispered back at him. 'Your way isn't working.'

'I've got a better way,' Jim told him. 'We'll get someone to follow him when he leaves. Hopefully he might lead us to Helen.'

Pleased at the prospect of some action at last, Paul said, 'All right. I'll do it.'

'No, not you. It has to be someone he hasn't met. Shane would do it.'

Paul could see the sense in this. 'I'll go and talk to him.' He jerked his head in the direction of the living room. 'You keep him busy.'

In the Ramsay house, Lucy had already told them what she knew of what was happening. 'Oh, Paul,' Madge said worriedly as Paul hurried into the kitchen. 'Lucy tells us—'

'Haven't got time to explain now, Madge.' He moved across to the table where Shane was polishing his boots on a sheet of newspaper. 'I need your help, mate.'

'Sure.' Shane put down the boot he had been polishing. 'This minister bloke?'

Paul nodded. 'I want you to follow him. Just see where he goes. He might lead us to Gran.'

'Do you reckon?' Shane looked doubtful. 'I mean, we're a bit old for this cops and robbers stuff, aren't we?'

'It's our only chance.'

'Why can't you go?'

'He knows me. He doesn't know you.'

'Why don't you leave it to the police?' Madge suggested.

'We haven't got time, Madge,' Paul told her. 'He's getting nervous.' He turned back to Shane. 'Well, what do you say?'

'I don't know. It all sounds a bit suss to me. But . . .' He stood up. 'I don't want to see Helen hurt. Okay, I'll do it.'

'I'll come with you,' Charlene said excitedly.

'Charlene!' Madge exclaimed. 'No!'

'He's got to have a partner,' Charlene returned. 'They always do on TV.'

Madge grimaced. 'So who's been watching too many late-night movies then?'

They were losing time. 'Come on, mate,' Paul urged Shane. 'I don't know how much longer Dad can hold him.'

'Yes, off you go,' Madge said.

Outside, Paul positioned Shane in the area between the two houses. From there, he would be able to see the Reverend Errol Price leave the Robinson house. 'Why would he be hanging around your place,' Shane wanted to know, 'if he's got something to do with Helen's disappearance?'

'I don't know.' Paul glanced over his shoulder to make sure Price was not already leaving. 'But he's the only clue we've got – so whatever you do, don't lose him. All right?'

'Don't worry, mate,' Shane assured him. 'I'll stick like glue.'

'Good. And give us a ring as soon as you know anything. I'll be at home.' He backed away a couple of steps. 'Now I'd better go.'

In the Robinson living room, the Reverend Errol Price was looking even more nervous. 'Oh, here he is,' Jim said quickly as Paul entered. 'I was just saying to the Reverend that you were having trouble loosening the nuts on the element . . .'

'That's right,' Paul said. 'Damn hard to get off. I had to go next door to borrow a pair of pliers.' He smiled briefly at the clergyman. 'Still working on it. Devil of a job. Won't take much longer.'

'It's all right, Paul.' As Errol Price glanced at his wristwatch, Paul nodded to his father to indicate that matters had been satisfactorily arranged. 'It's . . . ah . . . getting late, I see. And I do have an appointment.' It seemed to Paul, watching him, that he was in a state of some anxiety. 'I'm afraid I'll have to skip the tea.' He stood up. 'If you'll excuse me . . .'

As they watched him walk quickly down the street, shadowed by Shane and, to Paul's surprise, Charlene, who had emerged from the side of the house to follow him, it seemed more than ever before clear that the man's guilt was indisputable.

The fact that Charlene took it on herself to be involved in this adventure, after some initial opposition from Shane – 'But what looks more normal?' she had insisted, 'a couple going for a walk, or some guy skulking . . . ?' – proved to be a deciding factor in the satisfactory outcome of the affair. It was Charlene who whistled for a passing taxi when the reverend gentleman hailed one for himself, just as Shane was about to run back home to collect his motorbike for the pursuit; it was also Charlene who wielded the weapon that brought about the downfall of the Reverend Errol Price. Its clanging reverberation had echoed from all the headstones in the cemetery.

Later, when they had calmed down, Charlene and Shane described their traumatic adventure. They had followed Price into the cemetery. As he walked purposefully between the graves, they had concealed themselves behind the headstones. They followed him to an old shed at the far end of the cemetery, where he pulled out a piece of wood which he had used to barricade the door, and stepped inside.

Creeping up to the shed, they could hear Price's voice. He was going on and on, saying all sorts of horrible things. He talked about Terry, and how she had suffered; called Paul a murderer. Then they heard Helen's voice, sounding very strained as she told the man she was sorry for him because he was very, very sick.

They knew they had to get her out of there somehow. When Charlene failed to dissuade Shane from entering the shed, she found the spade lying on the ground near a newly-dug grave and had run quickly back to the shed with it.

Meanwhile Price had fought with Shane, knocked him down, then raced out of the shed – with Shane in hot pursuit – straight into the spade which Charlene had wielded with all her strength. At first she thought she had killed him.

'He was quite mad,' Helen said later, after she had been brought back home. 'He was so obsessed. He really intended to kill me. He wanted to make this family suffer.'

She described how he had lured her to the cemetery. He had visited the house the day before and talked about Terry, about guilt and humanity. He told Helen he wanted to pray at Terry's grave, and asked her to show him where it was . . . Helen had been completely taken in; she'd no reason to doubt his sincerity. It was only when they were at the graveside, having driven to the cemetery in Helen's car, that she had become alarmed. He began to act quite strangely, weeping uncontrollably. Helen had backed uneasily away, but he had stopped her. Almost incoherent by then, he kept calling Terry's name, declaring his love for her. He said he had vowed revenge on the man who had caused her death. He had then forced Helen into the shed where he had bound and gagged her.

Errol Price – or rather, Ralph Drew, which was his real name – was now in police custody. 'It was really me he wanted, wasn't it?' Paul asked miserably.

Responsibility. With Terry, what had started out as a dream had turned into a nightmare. Even now, from beyond the grave, she was still reaching out for him.

'No one's to blame, Paul,' Helen said gently. 'Ralph Drew is a very sick man.'

Eight

Madge Mitchell was not a woman who was easily surprised. She wasn't surprised now; she was more amused and highly sceptical about what she had just heard. She knew her father too well. 'Who'd like a cup of tea?' she asked.

'But, Mum.' Charlene was the one to show surprise. 'Didn't you hear what Granddad just said?'

Of course she had heard what her father had just said. He had told her he was in a position to make her a wealthy woman – and she didn't believe him. 'Your grandfather has a talent for dangling a carrot just before he delivers a lecture,' she said, filling the jug with water. 'I'm sure he's going to tell me to keep my mouth shut, my shoulder to the wheel, and my nose to the grindstone.'

'Not a pretty picture,' Dan Ramsay remarked drily.

'What do you *really* mean, Granddad?' Shane was staring at Dan. 'About making Auntie Madge a wealthy woman?'

'Just what I said. But as she's obviously not interested . . .'

'But she is,' Charlene said quickly. 'Aren't you, Mum?'

Madge had switched on the jug. She returned to the table where the others were sitting. 'In a word. No.'

'Well – ' Dan looked steadily up at his daughter who was just rejecting a small fortune. 'I was under the impression you were short of cash.'

Madge was setting out the cups and saucers. 'I wouldn't be short of cash,' she retorted, 'if that rotten son of yours paid me the money he owes me for the house in full instead of in dribs and drabs.'

'Is that it?' Shane queried excitedly. 'Has Dad come up with the money?'

'It's nothing to do with Max.' Reaching into his hip pocket, Dan produced an envelope. 'This is a letter from your Aunt Maud,' he informed Madge.

'She's dead,' Shane observed.

'I know she's dead, son,' Dan said shortly. 'She wrote this on her deathbed.' He brandished the envelope. 'Her Will's in here, too. Do you want me to read the letter, Maggie?'

Madge was thinking sourly of her Aunt Maud; it would be just like her to have the last word – even on her deathbed. 'No, you read it. It'll sound more like her that way.'

Extracting two sheets of paper from the envelope, Dan unfolded one of them. Then, after clearing his throat importantly, he began to read: '"My dear Madge, As you are aware, I have never really approved of you and your wild ways . . ."'

'Wild ways?' Charlene looked at her mother in amusement. 'Mum?'

'Your Great-Aunt Maud was a very narrow-minded woman,' Madge said primly.

Dan continued to read the letter. '"You are fortunate I have been able to find it in my heart to forget that disgraceful incident with the green frog . . ."'

'Oh, for God's sake,' Madge snorted. 'That damned green frog. That was more than thirty years ago.'

'What about the green frog, Auntie Madge?' Shane asked eagerly.

Madge didn't want to discuss the green frog. 'She hid it in Aunt Maud's nightgown,' Dan explained, to his daughter's embarrassment. 'The screams could be heard for miles.'

Charlene laughed. 'Oh, Mum!'

Madge glowered fiercely at her. 'Shut up, Charlene.'

'Can I continue?' Dan frowned up at them, then, when there was silence, resumed his reading of Aunt Maud's letter. '"You may remember how I warned you against marrying that no-hoper Fred Mitchell. As usual, I have been proved right. He left you for a younger woman, and . . ."'

'That does it.' Madge had heard enough; she was furious. That self-righteous, interfering old . . . 'Dad, you can tear up that letter.'

But Dan was still reading. '"Max and Tom have both grown into fine Ramsay men . . ."'

'She must have gone senile . . .'

'". . . and are obviously financially secure. For this reason, and also because you are my only niece, I am asking your father to decide if you deserve a legacy from me. Till we meet again,"' Dan concluded. '"Your dear departed Aunt Maud."' He dropped the letter onto the table and sat back with a self-satisfied smile.

The water had boiled. Madge busied herself by preparing the tea. 'Does this mean she's left Auntie Madge some money?' Shane enquired.

Dan nodded. 'How much?' Charlene wanted to know.

'It could be a lot of money. But then again, it could be nothing at all.' Now Dan's smile was enigmatic. 'It all depends.'

Madge brought the tray across to the table. 'Depends on what?'

Dan was clearly enjoying his role as the man of mystery. 'On whether I think it would be better spent as a memorial to the dear old lady,' he said. 'Some sort of set-up at a university – a foundation.' A far-away look came into his eyes as he thought about it. 'Yeah, why not?'

Madge chuckled softly as she poured the tea; she was beginning to find some humour in this situation after all. 'What kind of memorial could you get for a few dollars?'

Dan raised his eyebrows. 'Who's talking about a few dollars?'

'Well?'

'We're talking about thousands,' Dan said.

'How many thousands?'

'Fifty.'

Now Madge really was surprised. More than that, she was absolutely dumbfounded.

It was a lot of money all right, but the more she thought about it the more firm she was in her decision not to accept it.

When she made this known, Shane tried to make her see sense. 'It's fifty thousand dollars you're turning down, you know,' he said in an aggrieved voice.

'Yes, I know.'

'You've read the Will. All we have to do is prove that you deserve the money.'

'Oh, is that all?' Could he imagine how impossible that was going to be with an old goat like his grandfather acting as judge and jury, as had been stipulated in Aunt Maud's Will?

'You can see why Maud wasn't sure about her,' Dan remarked to Shane and Charlene. Then to Madge he said in a voice full of reproach, 'You . . . you're

. . . what's the word? Not unstable. No, unreasonable.'

Madge regarded him with a stony expression. 'Didn't you have to go out?'

'I do.'

'Then you'd better go.'

'No, Granddad.' Charlene clutched his arm as he was rising from his chair. 'We should talk about this. Now,' she went on as her grandfather sank back onto the chair, 'the Will states that you're the one who has to decide if Mum gets the money or not – is that right?'

'There *is* no decision,' Madge broke in before Dan could reply. She fixed her father with a baleful stare. 'You can take your miserable fifty thousand and give it to the university, or whatever. That's what you want to do, anyway.'

'Oh, Maggie.' Dan shook his head in sorrow. 'You've always misjudged me. I want *you* to have this money.'

'Then hand it over.'

'You know I can't do that. You read the Will. I owe it to the family name to make sure it's—' he glanced across at Charlene '—What's the word?'

'Perpetuated.'

'Perpetuated in an honourable way.' Dan leaned forward across the table. 'All Maud is asking is that you prove to me that she had misjudged you all those years.'

'And how is she supposed to do that?' Shane asked.

Dan smiled slowly. Inwardly flinching, Madge waited for the expected blow to fall. 'By showing me a gentle and loving side to her nature,' Dan said smoothly. 'By,' he shrugged, 'for this week, anyway, treating me with the respect I deserve.' He glanced at his wristwatch. 'Oh, goodness, is that the time?' He stood up. 'I'd better go. I'll be late for my appointment.' He turned back to his daughter, who was still trying to come to terms with what he had just put to her. 'Think about it, Maggie.'

'And don't call me Maggie!' Madge called angrily after him as he hurried out of the room.

Shane and Charlene continued to try and persuade her to change her mind. 'Mum, you have to do it,' Charlene insisted. 'We need the money.'

That was right; they needed the money – but at what cost to her self-respect? And in any case, Madge was quite convinced that her father had already made up his mind about how the money was to be dispersed. 'He wants it to go to a memorial foundation,' she said emphatically. 'Can't you see that? The Ramsay name is the only thing that matters. He'll give me hell for a week, then hand it all over to some university or other.'

Shane pleaded with her. 'Auntie Madge, we'll help you be . . . nice to him.'

'Yes.' Charlene nodded in agreement. 'If Gramps wants loving kindness for a week, then let's give it to him. Fifty thousand bucks worth.'

Madge was finding herself painfully torn. While she desperately needed the money, she was appalled by the idea of what she would have to do to receive it. 'I'll think about it,' she said with a sigh.

Dan hadn't told them where he was going; he had just mentioned an appointment, that was all. He was back in time for lunch. Madge decided to apply a little pressure.

'Dad,' she began tentatively. 'About Aunt Maud's Will. I really do need that money.'

'You know the conditions,' Dan said a little brusquely. 'You can't blame her for wanting to make sure you're no longer cackle-headed.'

Madge bridled at this. 'When was I ever . . . cackle-headed?' she demanded.

'Come off it, girl,' Dan snorted. 'You know how Aunt Maud and I begged you to marry Harold Bishop.' Madge groaned; Harold Bishop was a subject that just would not go away. 'If you'd married him, you'd be in clover now.'

'You mean six feet under?'

Dan was stung to defend the worthy Harold Bishop. 'He's got one of the best stock and station agencies in the State,' he said with a peeved expression. 'He's a smart man. Not like Fred Mitchell.'

Well, maybe . . . There was no way Fred could be described as smart. 'We all make mistakes, Dad,' Madge murmured.

'Yes, but you've been making them all your life.'

'Well, I'll do my best,' Madge said humbly, even though it almost choked her to say it.

Shane came in from outside. He looked at Dan in concern. 'You're not sick are you, Granddad?' he asked.

Dan was suddenly tense. 'Why do you say that?'

'Mrs Mangel said she saw you at Clive's surgery.'

Madge quickly picked up on this. 'What were you doing at Clive's surgery?' she queried.

'That's none of your business.' Rising to his feet, Dan moved across the room to confront Shane. 'And your grandmother must not be told one word of this,' he growled. 'You understand? Not one word,' he repeated as he stomped angrily out of the room.

Madge and Shane exchanged a puzzled glance. 'What did he have to see Clive about?' Madge asked.

Shane gave a shrug. 'Maybe he's just stacking on a turn to get his own way.'

I don't know—' Madge was suddenly worried; her

father *was* getting on in years. 'It could be something serious.'

'If it was,' Shane observed, 'he would hardly wait to tell us about it. No,' he shook his head. 'I think he's just trying to put one over you.'

Madge couldn't see why he would need to do that; she had already indicated to him that she would do her best to tow the line as far as Aunt Maud's legacy was concerned. 'I think he'll make you earn every cent of that money,' Shane said when she pointed this out to him. 'It will be like getting blood out of a stone.'

But Madge wasn't so sure. 'You can't be too careful,' she said, pushing back her chair. She stood up and moved across to the door. 'I think I'll go and have a chat with Clive.'

'What about Granddad's lunch?'

'Could you serve it up for him? I don't want him to be left alone until we find out what's wrong with him.'

But Clive, true to his professional ethics, wasn't forthcoming. 'I'm sorry, Madge,' he said with an unaccustomed air of seriousness, 'but I can't discuss your father's state of health without his consent.'

Which only served to increase Madge's concern. 'That sounds as if it's serious,' she said with a worried frown.

'I didn't say that.'

'He's really ill, isn't he?'

'Did he tell you that?' Clive asked warily.

'Not in so many words.'

'Well . . .' Clive regarded her thoughtfully for a moment. 'We're waiting for the results of some tests,' he told her. 'Until they come through, I don't know what's wrong with your father.'

'Clive, I've got to know what to expect. I'm his daughter.'

'I think you're jumping the gun a little,' Clive said calmly. 'All I can do is suggest you wait until the results come through. Then you can ask Dan to discuss it with you.'

He made it sound too easy. 'Dad can be as stubborn as a mule when he wants to be,' Madge said unhappily. 'Even if he *is* seriously ill, I'd be the last person he would tell.'

When she returned to the house, she nevertheless tried to get Dan to discuss his problem with her. She told him she had seen Clive. ''Strewth, Maggie,' he exclaimed. 'What did you do that for?'

'Because I'm worried about you.'

Dan gave her a scornful look. 'Pig's eye you are. All you care about is getting your hands on Aunt Maud's inheritance.'

'That's not true.' Madge was hurt by the accusation. 'Dad, if you've got a problem, I want to know what it is.'

'What did Clive have to say?' Dan asked cautiously.

'Nothing much,' Madge replied. 'But I had the impression there was something seriously wrong.'

Dan became angry. 'He had no right to blab.'

'Don't be ridiculous,' Madge retorted. 'Now are you going to tell me what's wrong, or do I have to drag it out of you?'

'I don't have to tell you anything,' Dan muttered.

Madge's voice was raised. 'Oh, you stubborn old goat!' she cried. 'I've got a good mind to . . . to . . .'

'You can call me what you like,' Dan broke in as she was still trying to think of something suitable to say. 'But you're not getting anything out of me. Including that money, if you're not careful.'

'Oh . . . oh . . .' Madge was totally fed up with him. 'You'll never change, will you? You've always been a cranky old man – and I'm beginning to think you were born that way. Honestly—' She shook her head in exasperation. 'How Mum puts up with you, I really don't know.'

'I don't mind getting my own way once in a while.' A crafty gleam appeared in Dan's eyes. 'But that's something *you'll* just have to put up with for the time being.' He winked at her. 'Isn't it, Maggie?'

Madge could quite easily have killed at that moment.

For dinner that evening she was preparing a savoury meatloaf. 'Can't stand meatloaf,' Dan complained when he discovered the source of the smell that was permeating the house. 'Gives me terrible indigestion.'

'You ate it last time you were here,' Shane reminded him.

'And look at the state I'm in now,' Dan said, with a meaningful glance at Madge.

Shane was watching his grandfather with a sober expression. 'I don't think there's anything wrong with you at all,' he said finally.

Dan scoffed at him. 'And you know everything, I suppose?'

'I know that you're giving Auntie Madge a hard time when she doesn't deserve one.'

'She'll be well rewarded when I'm gone,' Dan said with a shrug.

Madge had been checking the meatloaf. She turned away from the stove. 'Dad, for the last time,' she said earnestly, 'it's not the money I'm worried about. It's you.'

'That'll be the day.'

Shane frowned at him. 'Listen to yourself, Granddad,' he said impatiently. 'The only thing wrong with you is your over-active imagination.'

'I'll need one,' Dan returned shortly, with a nod in

Madge's direction, 'if I'm to believe a word that comes out of *her* mouth.'

Madge decided it was time to put a stop to this before it got out of hand. 'That's enough, Shane. Let your grandfather read his newspaper in peace.'

'But you can't be fooled by the way he's carrying on,' Shane muttered resentfully.

'I'll do what I think is best,' Madge briskly informed him. 'And I do think it would be a good idea if you stayed out of it.'

'Aw, I give up.' Shane made for the door. 'I'm going for a ride on my bike.'

'Don't be too long,' Madge called after him, then glanced coldly at her father. 'I'm putting some steaks on in a couple of minutes.'

Now Dan was definitely interested. 'You must want that money pretty badly, Maggie,' he said with a knowing smile.

She began to fuss over him; she was doing what she could, sometimes to his irritation, to make him comfortable. The following morning, she asked him if he would like anything special for dinner that night.

Dan thought about it. 'Some pickled pork would go down well,' he said at last.

Madge was dubious. 'I'm sure Clive wouldn't approve of that.'

'All right then,' he said testily. 'But make it anything but flamin' meatloaf. And don't fuss, woman. You're sounding more like your mother every day.'

'That's probably because we both care about you,' Madge responded. 'And speaking of Mum, I really think she should be told that you're not well.'

'What would be the point of that?' Dan countered. 'It's bad enough that *you're* having kittens without her having them as well.'

When Madge arrived home from work that evening,

she was startled to see a packed suitcase in the living room. Her father was standing beside it. 'Where are you going?'

'As if you care.'

Madge flared up at him. 'Of course I damn well care,' she cried. 'If you have to go to hospital, I have a right to know.'

'The only place I'm going is home,' Dan told her. 'I've seen Clive and the tests are clear. Just a mild irritation of the stomach lining, he said, nothing to worry about. All I've got to do is watch my diet . . .'

Madge almost threw her arms around him in her relief. 'Oh, Dad . . .' Then she thought of something. Her face clouded. 'Why didn't you call me as soon as you found out?'

Dan's expression was sullen. 'No concern of yours,' he muttered.

Madge was becoming angry again. 'You . . . you . . . oh, you horrible old man,' she accused him in a rising voice. 'I've gone out of my way to make things easy for you since you've been here, and you couldn't care less how I felt.'

Dan's face was set grimly as he returned her stare. 'You had fifty thousand reasons to make things easy for me, Maggie,' he said. 'And don't you forget it.'

Warmth rushed into Madge's cheeks. 'Do you *really* think that that's the kind of daughter you've raised?' she yelled. 'Do you think I'm being nice to you just to get hold of Aunt Maud's money?'

'Well, all right – ' Dan backed away from her uneasily. 'Hold your horses,' he muttered.

Madge was being carried along on the impetus of her rage. 'If that's what you think about me, then you can take your rotten money and . . . and . . .'

'All right, I will.' Dan turned abruptly away from her. 'Just as soon as I get out of this house.'

As he stomped off to his room, Madge's anger ebbed away and in its place came the awful, sickening realisation of what she had just done. That stupid money – she wished she had never heard about it; it had caused nothing but trouble. But, she told herself, they could still manage without it – they would have to manage without it. They had managed to keep the roof over their heads so far without his help, hadn't they? And they could go on doing it. What Dan did with Aunt Maud's money was his own business.

Carrying his other bag, Dan came back into the room. He put the bag down, and reaching into his pocket produced an envelope.

Madge eyed it suspiciously. 'What's this?'

'It'll cover my board.' Dan held the envelope out to her.

She snatched the envelope from him. 'Oh.' She shook her head in exasperation. What could she do with him? What could anyone do with him? 'You silly, stubborn old fool.' She was amused and irritated at the same time. 'You know you've always got a home here. It's got nothing to do with the money; it's because I love you.'

'Hang on, Maggie.' Dan nodded to the envelope she was holding in her hand. 'Take a look at what's inside.'

Puzzled, she opened the envelope. Inside was a cheque. She took it out from the envelope and studied it. She saw her name; she saw the amount. 'Oh, Dad—' She couldn't believe it. 'Fifty thousand . . .'

Dan smiled at her fondly. 'I reckon your mother and me can afford to advance it to you until old Maud's money comes through,' he said with a chuckle. 'I was always going to give it to you. I thought you would twig to that.'

Laughing and crying at the same time, she rushed

to him and threw her arms around him. 'Oh, Dad, you're a ratbag – you know that?'

'And I love you too, sweetheart,' Dan said with another chuckle, as he hugged her in return.

Nine

It was Des Clarke's birthday. Daphne was over at the Robinson house, helping Helen prepare cakes and things for some stupid school fête. Des didn't think that was right at all; he was much more important than any school fête. 'I'm going across there right now,' he said with grim determination.

'She'll be back soon,' Mike Young said quickly, positioning himself between Des and the door.

'I don't care.'

'Des . . .' Mike had reached the door ahead of him and was doing something frantic with the handle. 'It seems to be stuck.'

'Let me have a look.'

'No. You're not well.'

That was true; Des had woken up this morning feeling decidedly seedy. It was probably some bug he had picked up from somewhere. Mike had suggested he suck an ice-cube because that was what Clive Gibbons recommended to his patients. So far Des had sucked three.

'Actually, I'm feeling much better. That trick with the ice-cubes seems to work.' Pushing in front of Mike, he tried the door; it opened without any difficulty at all.

Jim and Lucy Robinson were standing on the doorstep. Lucy was holding a brightly gift-wrapped package. She thrust it at him. 'Happy birthday, Des,' she said chirpily.

'Happy birthday, mate,' Jim said.

'Oh, thank you.' Des took the package from Lucy. 'Thanks a lot. What is it?'

'Chocolate liqueurs,' Jim told him.

Des pulled a face; food was the very last thing he wanted to think about at the moment.

'Don't you like them?' Lucy was looking up at him inquiringly.

'Yeah.'

'You can eat them later then.'

Des nodded. 'I was just on my way to your place,' he told Jim. 'To see Daphne.'

'Oh, I wouldn't if I were you,' Jim said hastily. 'It's a madhouse over there. Waist-deep in chocolate crackles and toffee the last time I looked. That's why we came over here.'

'Yes.' Lucy nodded in agreement. 'Everybody's cooking.'

'Real ladies' day,' Jim remarked.

'They're even making a special cake,' Lucy said, then looked suddenly abashed.

'They're catering for three different stalls,' Jim explained with a quick glance at his daughter. 'Having the time of their lives. No, mate,' he shook his head. 'You're better off leaving them to it.'

'Why don't I make some tea?' Mike suggested.

Jim was swift to take him up on the offer. 'Good idea, Mike.'

'Yes, please,' Lucy said brightly.

'You'll have some, too, won't you, Des?' Mike said.

'Yeah, fine.' Des looked at Jim. 'So it's really that bad over there?'

'Worse,' Jim solemnly assured him.

Well, if it was so bad, Des thought glumly, then it was probably best to leave them to it. All the same, he couldn't help wondering about it.

'Why are Helen and Daphne doing all this cooking?' he asked while they waited for the jug to boil.

'They're the best cooks, I guess,' Jim opined.

'It's not only them,' Lucy chimed in. 'Your Mum's there as well.'

'Mum?' Des was surprised. 'She hasn't had anything to do with that school for years,' he said. 'Kids make her nervous. They give her the horrors.'

'She probably enjoys re-living old school fêtes,' Jim suggested.

Not his mother. Definitely not his mother. 'That's not the way her mind works,' Des said with a shake of his head.

'I know the real reason she's over there,' Lucy said.

Jim frowned. 'I don't think we need your theories, Lucy,' he muttered tersely.

'It couldn't be any worse than yours, mate,' Des said. 'What do you reckon, Lucy?'

'Because she got her voice back, and she just wants to talk.'

That was more like it. 'Got it in one, Lucy,' Des said with a chuckle. 'You don't miss a thing, do you? Don't miss a trick.'

The more he thought about it, the more puzzled he was by Daphne's behaviour. 'It's my birthday,' he complained as they sipped their tea. 'I'm sick, and she's out cooking for an entire school fête. And we don't have any kids.' He looked forlornly across the table at Jim Robinson. 'Wouldn't you be a bit annoyed if you were me?'

'We all make commitments, Des,' Jim replied with an easy shrug. 'Daphne just likes to keep to hers.'

Des couldn't see the point to that at all. 'What's her biggest commitment?' he demanded. 'Me or the school fête?'

'Well,' Jim said thoughtfully, 'I suppose that's one way of putting it . . .'

Des turned to the little girl. 'Lucy, when is this fête?'

'Well . . .' Lucy thoughtfully bit her lower lip. 'Next Saturday.'

'At the school or the reserve?'

'The school, I think.'

'You think? You don't know?'

'The school.'

'Right.' Des put down his cup. 'That gives the real mothers one full week to make toffee and chocolate crackles for this high priority happening. What's the money for, anyway?' he asked.

Jim and Mike answered simultaneously. 'Sports equipment,' Jim said, as Mike said it was for maths equipment.

'Sports *and* maths equipment,' Jim and Lucy chorused.

This didn't sound right to Des. 'They spent a fortune on sports equipment last year,' he recalled. 'They've got an account at the bank.' He remembered something else. 'Come to think of it, the fête wasn't held at this time last year. Yes . . . They came into the bank with these huge bags of coins. It took us ages to count it, even with the machine.'

Lucy quickly changed the subject. 'Des, you do want me to have a good education, don't you?'

'Of course I do, sweetheart,' Des replied. 'But I can't see what Daphne having to cook for the fête has to do—'

'Then let's play Scrabble,' Lucy interrupted him

with a hopeful smile. 'It would help me learn more words.'

'Good idea,' Jim said.

Mike, too, thought it was a good idea. Des thought they were all crazy. 'It's a beautiful Sunday morning,' he said in a tone of wonder, 'and you guys want to play *Scrabble*?'

Jim nodded.'If it will help Lucy's education . . .'

'And I've always liked Scrabble,' Mike said with enthusiasm.

Lucy's eyes were wide and expressive as she gazed at Des. 'Please, Des.'

Des gave in, but he was still doubtful. 'All right. If that's what you want.'

Mike was on his feet. 'I'll get the board,' he said.

They played Scrabble. Des was feeling much better now. He was also feeling very hungry; he had a sudden craving for some banana custard. 'Anyone else want some?' he asked from the refrigerator.

'No, thanks,' Jim said. 'You go right ahead.'

Mike looked up from the Scrabble board. 'I thought you were feeling sick.'

'The ice worked wonders,' Des told him. 'And I had a sudden craving for banana custard.' He peered into the refrigerator. 'And I've got some gherkins. Anyone want a gherkin?'

'With banana custard?' They were all staring at him in amazement.

'Well . . .' Des shrugged. 'Just a thought.'

Charlene Mitchell came in through the back door. 'Mister Robinson is wanted back home,' she announced, after greetings had been exchanged.

With a sigh, Jim stood up. 'I'm afraid duty calls, old son,' he said to Des. 'I'll leave you to it.'

'I'll be over in a minute,' Des told him as he walked to the door.

'I wouldn't, if I were you,' Charlene said.

'Why not?'

'Your Mum's taken over.' Charlene sat down on the chair that had just been vacated by Jim Robinson. 'She's got them all working like slaves.'

The door closed behind Jim. It was Des's turn to make a move on the Scrabble board, but his mind was on other things. He headed once more for the refrigerator; those gherkins had looked too tempting.

Lucy won the game. 'That makes me the champion then,' she said, standing up. 'I think I'll go home now.'

'I'll come with you,' Des said.

Lucy frowned uncertainly. 'Ah . . . well . . . actually I said I'd go to a friend's place.' The frown cleared. 'So I think I'll go there.'

The telephone rang. Mike answered it as Des began to pack up the Scrabble game. He grunted a few times then hung up. 'Who was that?' Des asked, biting into another gherkin.

'Um . . . it was Daphne.' Mike glanced at Charlene with whom he had been quietly conversing. 'She . . . she's worried about you being sick. She thinks you should see Clive.' Charlene supported this with an eager nod.

'I'm okay.' Des studied the gherkin he was holding with distaste. 'I don't know why I eat these things. They're really quite vile.'

'She was pretty determined about it,' Mike said.

'Really?' Des gave him a dry look. 'That's nice to hear.'

'She *is* worried about you,' Charlene said fervently.

'Okay, okay.' Des gestured impatiently. 'But I don't need Clive. I'll go over to the Robinsons and tell Daphne I'm okay.'

'No, Des,' Mike protested. 'She wouldn't want that.'

Just what the hell *was* going on here? It was almost as if there were a deliberate campaign afoot to keep him away from the Robinson house. And now they wanted him out of *this* house. It was all very peculiar. 'What's up with you guys?' Abruptly, he pushed himself up out of his chair. 'I tell you, I'm going . . .'

The giddiness struck him in relentlessly strengthening waves. He clutched the table; he felt clammy and cold and sank back onto his chair. 'Des,' he could only just hear Charlene crying out in alarm, 'are you okay?'

They were pushing his head between his knees; he could hardly breathe. He began to wave his arms about. 'Let go, Mike,' he said in a muffled voice.

Mike was still pushing his head down. 'Just breathe normally – all right?'

'I *can't* breathe.'

'Shall I get Clive?' Charlene asked.

'He should be okay,' Mike said.

Des continued to struggle. 'Let go!' he yelped. Then, as the pressure was suddenly relaxed, something wet and cold was slapped on to the back of his neck. Des sprang up. He glared belligerently at Mike. 'What were you trying to do?' he snapped. 'Suffocate me?'

Mike was looking a little shamefaced. 'Well . . .'

Des plucked the wet tea towel from his neck and, holding it at arm's length, examined it critically. 'What's this?'

'You fainted,' Mike explained. 'I was trying to get the blood back to your head.'

'My blood was fine. It was the air in the lungs that was the trouble.'

'I'm sorry.' Mike gestured helplessly. 'It usually works.'

'You had us worried,' Charlene said.

'I stood up too quickly,' Des said, 'that's all.'

'Well?' Mike asked him. 'How do you feel now?'

'When I get my breath back, I'll let you know.'

Mike and Charlene exchanged a glance. 'You should definitely go and see Clive,' Mike said earnestly to Des.

Charlene added her support to this proposal. 'It's not normal to faint from just standing up, you know.'

'That's right,' Mike nodded to Des. 'I knew a guy once who fainted every time he stood up.'

'What happened to him?'

'He died.'

'I'm getting a headache.' Des clasped a hand to his forehead. 'Maybe you should bring Clive over here.'

'No!' Charlene exclaimed. 'I mean . . . ,' she appealed to Mike '. . . isn't exercise good for the circulation?'

Mike nodded. 'The walk will do you good,' he said to Des.

'But I'm sick.'

They began to lift him out of the chair. 'No, you're fine,' Mike assured him.

Carefully, one on each side of him, they led him to the door.

When Clive Gibbons jokingly offered him a lollipop because, as he said, he offered all his young patients lollipops, he was surprised when Des, brightening up considerably, accepted it.

Mike and Charlene had left him there, after explaining to Clive – mostly out of Des's hearing – what had happened. Clive was just about to check his blood pressure when he offered him the lollipop.

'Well?' Des asked after his blood pressure had been taken, sucking happily.

'It appears to be normal.'

'Terrific.' Des prepared to rise. 'Then I'll be going.'

Clive pushed him back onto the chair. 'I'll need to keep you under observation for a couple of hours.'

Des was suddenly worried again. 'Do you think it's serious?' he asked, searching Clive's face for any sign to indicate how serious it might be.

'I doubt it,' Clive replied thoughtfully. 'I just want to be sure, that's all.' He stood up. 'Now, can I get you anything? Coffee? Tea?'

Des had finished his sweet. 'Have you got another lollipop?'

Clive shook his head regretfully. 'That was my last one. Sorry.'

'A pickled onion then?' Des asked with an expression of hope.

While he waited at Clive's he watched the tennis on television. Then, suddenly, after about an hour, Clive was propelling him to the door. He began to protest; he had become quite comfortable sitting in Clive's living room and watching the tennis. 'But I thought you wanted to keep an eye on me. In case it was something serious.'

'It's not serious,' Clive assured him as he ushered him along the hall to the front door. 'And the best place to recuperate is in your home.'

'But I was watching the tennis.'

'You'll enjoy it more at your place.'

'But it's my birthday. I should be with people.'

Clive opened the front door. 'You can be with Daphne.'

'But Daphne's at the Robinsons,' Des gloomily informed him, 'up to her eyeballs in chocolate crackles.'

Outside, Paul Robinson was just reaching into his car for something when Des hailed him. He straightened, turned, and when he recognised Des looked momentarily awkward. He was holding something behind his back. 'Ah . . . Des. How are you?'

Des nodded towards Clive. 'Ask the doctor.'

'I'm just taking him home,' Clive said.

Now that they had run into Paul, Des had a suggestion to make. 'Why don't we go down to the Waterhole and celebrate?'

'Celebrate what?' Paul looked at him blankly.

'It's his birthday,' Clive explained. 'But he should be home,' he added pointedly. 'Right now.'

'Yeah,' Paul said ruefully. 'Another time, Des.'

Des was disappointed. 'Sure.' Then, noticing the package Paul was holding behind his back, his mood lightened. 'Ah, so you did remember then?' He pointed to the package.

'No, I didn't,' Paul said quickly, no longer making an effort to conceal the package. 'This is for Lucy.'

The disappointment descended again. 'Yeah,' Des muttered. 'I knew that. Sure thing.'

'For Christmas,' Paul said, as Des and Clive passed him on their way to the Clarke house. 'Thought I'd get in before the rush.'

The house was empty when they entered, Clive allowing Des to go ahead of him – and then, suddenly, it wasn't. People were coming out from everywhere – from rooms and cupboards, from behind armchairs and curtains, to grin at him, applaud him and wish him a happy birthday. There was a lot of shouting and laughing and people clapped him warmly on the back. Des was overcome by it all; he felt quite choked up about it. He noticed the streamers and balloons that had been tacked up around the place. So that was what it had been about, all the preparations over at the Robinsons, making believe it was for a school fête, all the comings and goings, keeping him away from the Robinsons, then getting him out of the house so they could set everything up for their surprise party. He experienced a rush of warmth towards these people, his neighbours, his friends, who had gone to so much trouble to surprise him on his birthday. Even Mrs Mangel was there.

There was food and drink; there were presents to open. 'There you are,' Clive said, handing him a tiny package. 'Many happy returns.'

'What is it?'

'Open it and find out.'

Des unwrapped the package to reveal an old silver coin. 'Hey, that's my lucky sixpence!' he exclaimed.

'Not at all,' Clive said. 'It's the lucky coin of the Gibbons family. It's been handed down from father to son for generations. It goes back to the early eighteenth century.'

'That's funny.' Des peered at the coin in the palm of his hand. 'It's got the date nineteen-forty-three.'

'Ah, yes.' Clive began to move away. 'There's a very interesting story attached to that.'

Daphne came up to them. Des kissed her. 'Have you had anything to eat?' she asked.

'I am a bit hungry, Daph,' Des told her.

'I'll get you something. What do you want?'

'Um—' Des hesitated. 'Pickled onions.'

'Pickled onions?' Daphne looked at him in surprise. 'But you hate them.'

'Not since I got sick.'

'They must be full of vitamins,' Daphne observed thoughtfully. 'I must be catching your disease, whatever it is,' she went on after a brief pause. 'I've also been eating pickled onions all day.'

Standing next to them, Clive suddenly looked very interested.

When the time came for him to cut the birthday cake, Des noticed that Daphne was nowhere to be seen. 'Make your wish, Desmond,' his mother said as she lit the candles.

Everyone was grouped expectantly around him and the cake but there was still no sign of Daphne. 'Hang on, Mum. Where's Daphne?'

'You'll have to start without her,' Eileen said, glancing around the room. 'Come on, the candles are melting.'

Des looked at the candles happily blazing away in their bed of icing. There seemed to be an awful lot of them. He was still concerned about Daphne. 'Hey, did anyone see where Daphne went?' he asked the room at large.

Nobody seemed to have any idea; there were negative murmurs. 'Just cut the cake, Des,' Lucy Robinson urged impatiently.

Then, to his relief, Daphne came into the room with Clive Gibbons. They were both smiling. Daphne hurried to Des's side. 'Where have you been?' he demanded in a low voice.

'Later, Des,' she whispered back.

Closing his eyes, Des blew out the candles in one attempt. There was an enthusiastic round of applause and some cheers. 'Make a wish, Desmond,' Eileen said with an approving smile. Des made a wish; it was an old wish. 'Now you can cut the cake.'

But as he was picking up the knife, Clive Gibbons called for everyone's attention. With some dismay, Des thought he was about to make a speech. 'I don't think that's necessary, Clive,' he murmured.

'Just listen to him, Des.' Daphne took his hand. 'It's important.'

Clive began to speak. 'I think you all know what Des wished for,' he said, beaming around the room. 'So, in my capacity as the magical medical magician, I hereby grant him that wish.' He turned to Des. 'Yes, my friend, by the symptoms you've been suffering, I pronounce you sympathetically pregnant.'

There was a gasp, then a cheer. Eileen kissed her son who could barely take in what he had just heard. 'That's wonderful, Desmond. I knew you could do it.' She was bubbling with happiness.

Des stared at Daphne who smiled back at him. 'It's true,' she said softly. 'We're going to have a baby.'

'Oh, Daph.' He hugged her, then, fearing he might cause some damage, sprang back again. 'Daph, that's wonderful!' He grinned at Clive. 'Thanks for that, Clive.' He raised his voice joyfully. 'We're actually having a baby.'

'You should remind me to give you a biology lesson one day,' Clive remarked drily.

Des was ecstatic; it was the best birthday present any man could have wished for. Everyone was happy for him and Daphne. Toasts were proposed. With tears of joy in his eyes, Des's own toast was to his beautiful wife and his wonderful, wonderful neighbours.

Ten

Could Mrs Mangel really have committed murder most foul? Was it possible that she would go down in the annals as the Ramsay Street Butcher? It certainly seemed very much to be the case.

Charlene Mitchell had heard Mrs Mangel screaming at her husband that afternoon. Death had been mentioned. 'I could kill you for what you've done, Len Mangel,' her thin voice had wailed from behind the brick veneer wall of her house. 'I could kill you!'

In the evening, Jane Harris arrived home to find her grandmother in a state of shock. Surrounded by upturned furniture and broken glass on the floor, she was sitting motionless in the living room, her eyes staring unseeingly. Jane was aghast; something terrible must have happened. She had never seen her grandmother looking like this before.

Charlene had told her about the argument, and Jane had resigned herself to a tense household when she arrived home. Her grandparents were always fighting, but nothing like this had ever happened in the past. There was no sign of her grandfather. 'Nan!' she cried in alarm as she ran to Mrs Mangel's side. 'What happened?'

But there was no response from Mrs Mangel; she

continued to sit there, staring blankly in front of her. Jane pleaded with her to say something, but Mrs Mangel remained silent. Jane became very frightened.

She needed help. She ran across the street to Clive Gibbons' house, but he wasn't home. Then she tried the Robinsons. To her great relief, Jim Robinson was in.

'Something terrible has happened, Mister Robinson. Please come.' She was struggling to catch her breath. Looking very concerned, Helen Daniels joined them in the hall. Lucy Robinson's head appeared in the dining-room doorway. 'Nan's just sitting there,' Jane gasped. 'There's broken glass all over the floor and . . . and I can't find Granddad.'

'We'd better see if she's all right,' Helen Daniels said worriedly to her son-in-law.

'I'll fetch Clive.' Jim strode out onto the porch. 'She might need him.'

'He's not there.' Jane was quite frantic. 'Please come. She looks terrible.'

Lucy stepped out into the hall. 'Can I come?' she asked hopefully.

'No, you can't,' Jim said firmly.

'You can finish setting the table,' Helen instructed her. 'We'll only be a few minutes.'

Lucy pouted. 'It's not fair,' she complained as they began to hurry down the path. 'I'm always the last to find out what's happening.'

There was another shock for Jane as she re-entered the Mangel house with Jim and Helen close behind her. Instead of finding the living room in a shambles and her grandmother in a daze, everything had been restored to its proper place and Mrs Mangel was sitting quite calmly in the same armchair, dabbing at a small cut on her hand with some cotton wool.

'Nell, are you all right?' Helen Daniels asked her.

Looking up at them, it seemed to take Mrs Mangel a moment or two to bring them into focus. 'Oh, good evening, Mrs Daniels.' She nodded to Jim. 'Mister Robinson.' She seemed quite composed.

Her mouth open, Jane was still staring dazedly around the living room which had been restored to normal. 'What seems to be the problem?' Jim queried gently.

'I beg your pardon?' Mrs Mangel gazed blandly up at him.

'Jane seemed to think there had been some sort of accident,' Jim explained.

Mrs Mangel looked reproachfully at Jane with eyes that still appeared a little glazed. 'What on earth made you think that?' She was fast returning to her old self.

Jane was totally confused by now. At one moment there had been a mess; now there was no mess at all. 'When I came home before . . . there was such a mess! I saw it.' She shook her head helplessly. 'I mean, you must have cleaned it up.' It was the only explanation possible.

Mrs Mangel regarded her unflinchingly. 'If you mean the old chair your grandfather broke,' she said, 'I took it out into the shed. My husband is always so clumsy,' she explained to Jim and Helen. 'Two left feet. I've often—'

'But there was broken glass on the floor!' Jane cried, moving quickly across to the standard lamp which earlier had been lying on its side and was now upright again. The glass shade of the lamp was broken. Jane pointed to it. 'See?'

Nor was there any glass in the cabinet doors. Jim was frowning down at something on one of the side tables. Then, tentatively, he touched his finger to it. He thoughtfully examined the tiny red spot on the tip of his finger. Mrs Mangel dabbed more energetically at the cut on her hand; she seemed to be suddenly agitated. 'The lamp was something else Len knocked over,' she said quickly. 'Of course I cleaned up the broken glass . . .'

Jane faced her. 'You and Granddad had a fight,' she said in an accusing tone.

'Fight?' Mrs Mangel's eyes flickered away from her grand-daughter.

'But you've cut yourself,' Helen said, moving forward. 'Let me see.' She reached out her hand.

Hastily, Mrs Mangel placed her other hand over the injured one. 'It's nothing. It's just a scratch. I must have nicked it on the broken glass.'

Jim glanced at the table which had the drop of blood on it. 'Is Mister Mangel home?' he asked.

'No . . .' Mrs Mangel's voice had become vague. 'He's gone away – a business trip.'

Jane looked at her sharply. 'He didn't say anything to me about a business trip.'

'It was at the last moment.' Mrs Mangel seemed to be pulling herself together as she spoke. 'One of the other sales representatives came down with a virus.' She glanced up at Helen. 'I don't know what nonsense Jane has been telling you, but it does seem that she has let her imagination run away with her.' She smiled a little tightly. 'I do appreciate your concern, but really, I'm perfectly all right.'

Helen glanced uncertainly at Jim. 'Are you sure there's nothing we can do?' she asked Mrs Mangel.

'No, no.' Mrs Mangel pushed herself up out of the armchair. 'Nothing at all, thank you.' She turned to Jane. 'I think you owe Mister Robinson and Mrs Daniels an apology,' she said coldly, 'for worrying them unnecessarily.'

It was more to placate her grandmother that Jane

did offer an apology. 'I guess it was a false alarm,' she said after she had done so.

'That's quite all right, Jane,' Helen said with a reassuring smile. 'It's better to be certain about these things.'

'I'll show you out,' Mrs Mangel said to Jim and Helen as she headed for the door.

Jane was thoroughly bewildered. There was something here that was not quite right, no matter what explanations her grandmother might have to offer. For instance, there was her grandfather's electric razor which was still in its accustomed place in the bathroom. 'I expect he forgot it in his rush to get away,' Mrs Mangel said, when Jane challenged her with this. 'Never mind. I suppose he'll buy some of those disposable ones.'

Jane was still trying hard to get at the truth. 'Nan, are you absolutely sure that Granddad went away on business? I mean, you weren't just saying that in front of Mister Robinson and Mrs Daniels, were you?'

'Of course not,' Mrs Mangel replied sharply.

'It's just that Charlene overheard you arguing . . .'

Mrs Mangel winced and closed her eyes as if intent on banishing an unpleasant memory. Then she opened her eyes again. 'Is that what made you bring the Robinsons over here?'

'I was worried about you,' Jane replied. 'You seemed . . . sort of . . . like you were in some sort of trance. Like shell shock, you know?'

'Oh, really, Jane.' Mrs Mangel studied her granddaughter with profound disapproval. 'What will the neighbours think if you go running to them with these wild stories?'

'But . . . the furniture . . . the broken glass?'

'I told you how it happened,' Mrs Mangel said crisply. 'That was just how it was.'

'But where did Granddad go?' Jane persisted.

'Now where did he say . . . ?' Mrs Mangel had all the appearance of a woman trying to recall what she had been told. She gave up the attempt. 'Oh, I've forgotten. He left in such a rush.'

'He always leaves the name of the hotel where he's staying beside the telephone,' Jane pointed out.

'No, I don't recall that he did this time,' Mrs Mangel said distantly. She sighed. 'Oh, Jane, please stop worrying. Everything is going to be all right.'

Jane tried to recall the names of the hotels where her grandfather usually stayed during his business trips, and even after she had checked the Yellow Pages was unable to come up with anything. She did think of something else, though, that turned out to be a little more positive.

'I've just called the garage where Granddad's car was in for service,' she told her grandmother. 'They told me it's still there.'

But Mrs Mangel had an answer for that one as well. 'He must be using a company car. He sometimes does, you know.'

Jane was becoming increasingly frustrated. 'I just want to talk to him, Nan,' she said desperately, 'and make sure he's okay. So, please, tell me what happened.'

'Nothing happened,' Mrs Mangel said very definitely. 'Nothing at all.'

Later that evening, Helen Daniels paid another visit to check on Mrs Mangel's condition. She also had another reason for being there. 'I think there's a job that might be of interest to you,' she told Jane, after Mrs Mangel had assured her that she was feeling quite fine.

'Oh?' Jane was definitely interested; she had been

looking for a job since she left school and wasn't finding it easy.

'In my office,' Helen said. 'I've talked it over with Paul, and he agrees that we could use some extra help.'

Jane beamed at her happily. 'That would be fantastic,' she exclaimed.

'The salary won't be enormous,' Helen said. 'And it will only be for a few weeks.'

That didn't matter in the slightest to Jane; she was delighted with the news that she had a job at last, even if it was only temporary. 'Nan . . .' She wanted to include Mrs Mangel in her excitement.

But her grandmother was standing by the window, and her face had that same blank expression Jane first noticed when she arrived back home that evening, and once or twice since then. 'Nan . . . are you all right?'

Mrs Mangel blinked a few times as if she were emerging from a trance, then quickly shook her head. 'A slight migraine,' she said listlessly. 'I think I'll go to bed. Goodnight.'

'She's been acting strangely,' Jane told Helen after Mrs Mangel had gone to her room. 'All of a sudden, she just goes blank.'

'Perhaps you could get Clive to have a look at her,' Helen suggested.

Jane shook her head. 'She wouldn't agree to that.'

'Then your grandfather – why don't you call him? I mean, he probably knows what has upset her.'

He probably did – but where was he? 'She won't tell me where he's staying. And . . . and . . .' It had almost become a certainty in Jane's mind. 'I don't think he's gone on a business trip at all.'

Helen looked at her closely. 'Where is he then?'

If only she knew. It was a question to which Jane herself was desperately trying to find an answer. 'He must have taken off,' she said unhappily. 'I think they had a terrible fight and . . . Well, I just hope he'll calm down and come home later tonight.'

Perhaps he would; she could only hope. Helen was watching her sympathetically. 'Are you sure there's nothing I can do?'

'Thanks.' Jane smiled at her a little wanly. 'Nan doesn't like anyone to know that she and Granddad don't get along. You won't tell anyone, will you?'

'No, of course not,' Helen assured her. 'But I want you to promise me one thing. If he *does* come home, and things are a bit tense, don't sit here worrying about it. You're welcome at our place any time.'

'Thanks, Mrs Daniels,' Jane said warmly. 'I'll remember that.'

When she was awakened that night by a loud clanging sound in the house, Jane's first thought was that her grandfather had returned home at last. Flinging back the bedclothes, she sprung out of bed and padded across to the bedroom door in her bare feet.

The hallway was in darkness. She could hear someone moving around in the living room which was also in darkness. 'Is that you, Granddad?' Reaching the door of the living room, she switched on the light.

But it wasn't her grandfather who stood there in the middle of the living room, blinking at her in surprise. It was her grandmother – and she had that dazed look again. There was dirt on the hem of her dressing gown and on the gumboots she was wearing; it was also on the spade she was holding. Presumably she had knocked it against something when she came into the house from wherever she had been. 'Nan, what's going on?'

'Jane.' Mrs Mangel seemed puzzled. 'What are you doing up at this hour?'

'Well . . . I thought I heard Granddad.'

'He won't be coming home tonight,' Mrs Mangel said flatly.

Jane nodded to the dirt-encrusted spade. 'What were you doing?'

Mrs Mangel looked down at the spade in some surprise, as if she didn't realise she was holding it. Then, with a confused shake of her head, she propped it against the wall. She opened her mouth to say something, then shook her head again.

'You must have been outside,' Jane prompted her. 'Don't you remember?'

'Outside,' Mrs Mangel whispered. 'The garden . . . I had to go into the garden.'

'You'd better go back to bed, Nan,' Jane said, taking her by the arm and leading her into the hall. 'You must have been walking in your sleep.'

'Yes,' Mrs Mangel said in a hollow, faraway voice. 'I suppose I must have been . . .'

In the morning, when she came into the kitchen in her dirt-smeared drssing gown, Mrs Mangel was appalled when Jane, in reply to her question, told her that it was already after eight.

'Oh dear,' she said with a frown. 'You should have woken me. I must have slept right through the alarm.' She seemed more in command of herself this morning. 'I had such a dreadful night, tossing and turning.'

'Oh, Nan!' Jane stared at her grandmother. 'Don't you remember?'

'Remember what?'

'Last night. You were walking in your sleep.'

'Don't be ridiculous,' Mrs Mangel snorted loftily. 'I've never done such a thing.'

'I heard a noise,' Jane told her slowly. 'I thought it was Granddad coming home. I came out to investigate. But it wasn't Granddad, it was you. You had been digging in the garden.'

A look of horror passed fleetingly across Mrs Mangel's face. Maybe she did remember after all, Jane thought. Then the look was gone, and Mrs Mangel's face was closed again. 'Why on earth would I do a thing like that?'

'I don't know.'

'It's totally absurd.'

'Just take a look at your dressing gown.' Jane stood up and turned to the door. 'And you had a spade. I'll show you.'

'No!'

Startled by the alarm in her grandmother's voice, Jane turned back to face her. 'I'm not making it up, Nan,' she said earnestly.

'I remember now.' Mrs Mangel's brow was furrowed in thought; she spoke deliberately. 'I bought some fertiliser yesterday. I didn't get a chance to put it on the garden. When I couldn't sleep . . . I thought I might as well spend some time in the garden.'

In the middle of the night? 'Couldn't it have waited?' Jane asked in astonishment.

'Yes. But now it's done.' Her voice began to drift away again; her eyes began to glaze. 'Over and done with . . .'

Helen Daniels was at work. Jane decided to turn to Madge Mitchell for help. Charlene answered the door. Kelly Morgan was with her. 'Charlene, is your mother home?'

'She's having a shower.'

'Would you ask her to come over to my place when she's ready.'

'What for?'

'It's Nan. She's acting really strange.'

'So what's new?' Kelly remarked drily. There was no love lost between her and Mrs Mangel.

'Shut up, Kelly.' Charlene looked steadily at Jane. 'What's the problem?' she asked.

Jane told them. She told them about her missing grandfather and her grandmother's strange behaviour. She told them everything. 'Sounds like she's gone round the bend,' Charlene observed when she had finished.

'Either that, or she's playing it real smart,' Kelly said with a knowing expression. 'Well, think about it,' she offered when they both looked at her. She addressed Jane. 'Your grandparents don't get on – right? They have a big fight. Then your Nan starts acting weird and hides the evidence. Your Granddad vanishes into thin air – and your Nan buries something in the back yard in the dead of night.' She gave a smug smile. 'Makes perfect sense to me.'

Jane was shocked. Her grandmother, in the middle of the night . . ? 'Nan wouldn't—'

Charlene echoed her thoughts. 'Mrs Mangel wouldn't do a thing like that.'

Kelly shrugged. 'You come up with a better idea then,' she said offhandedly.

There was a weighty silence as they searched in vain for a better explanation, then Charlene said, 'Maybe we should look in the garden. Just to be sure.'

Jane flinched from the suggestion. 'No.' She glared at Kelly who had just planted all sorts of worrying seeds of suspicion.

'Suit yourselves then,' Kelly said casually. 'But you'll never know otherwise.'

Charlene looked sombrely at Jane. 'She's right, you know,' she said. 'Come on, it couldn't hurt just to take a look.'

Terrified at the thought of what they might find buried in the back garden, Jane nevertheless followed them reluctantly as they headed towards her grandmother's house.

'This is ridiculous,' she protested as they stealthily made their way into the back garden, where it was all very still and quiet.

Frowning at her, Kelly raised her finger to her lips. 'Do you want the old bat to hear us?' she warned.

Jane had brought the spade outside that morning and left it against the wall of the house. Kelly took hold of it. 'Now what?' Charlene asked her.

'First we look for signs of disturbance. Then we dig.'

They began to search among the azaleas and grevilleas, the fuchsias and native plants that made Mrs Mangel's back yard so colourful.

'Charlene, this is crazy,' Jane said nervously. 'If Nan comes out and catches us . . .'

'Over here,' Kelly called in a low, urgent voice.

She was standing beside a freshly-turned mound next to the back fence. 'What's this?'

'A mound of compost,' Jane told her.

'Wrong.' Kelly shook her head. 'It's a mound of earth, made to look like a mound of compost.' She held the spade out to Charlene. 'Start digging,' she commanded.

Charlene looked doubtfully at the spade, then at Kelly. 'Don't look at *me*,' she muttered. 'This was all your idea.'

'I supplied the brains,' Kelly returned. 'Someone else can do the manual labour.'

Jane stepped forward. 'I'll do it.'

'No, Jane.' Charlene took the spade from Kelly. 'You'll get yourself dirty. I'll do it.'

Charlene began to dig into the mound of soil, and almost immediately the spade struck something solid. Charlene and Jane looked fearfully back at Kelly who was suddenly not looking so sure of herself. 'She should have buried him a bit deeper than that,' she said, adopting an air of disapproval. 'One good shower and the whole thing would—'

'Can you stop talking like that,' Jane broke in tensely, 'and see what it is.'

'Okay.' Bending forward, Kelly tentatively began to brush away the dirt with the edge of her hand as Jane, her hand clapped to her mouth, stepped away to distance herself from the discovery she was quite convinced would be gruesome.

But it wasn't gruesome; it was an old mantel clock. Jane, on being urged to open her eyes because what had been unearthed wasn't what she had thought it was, recognised it immediately. 'Hey, that's Nan's,' she cried in surprise. 'Granddad gave it to her when they were married.'

Both Kelly and Charlene looked perplexed as they studied the clock. 'Why would she want to chuck it away?' Charlene asked.

Jane had no idea; she was just as bewildered as they were. 'I don't know,' she murmured.

Charlene was examining the hole that had been dug in the soil. Kelly grimaced at the clock in distaste. 'I don't blame her for wanting to toss it away,' she said.

There was a cry from Charlene. 'Hey, there are more things here, clothes and stuff, and . . . oh yuk!'

Kelly and Jane stared down at the dentures that had just gone spinning out of Charlene's rummaging hand to land on the dirt a short distance away. 'Looks like your Granddad's teeth got the old heave-ho, too,' Kelly observed with an expression of awe.

'That's his spare set.' Jane looked at the clothes that had been partially unearthed. 'Yes, they're his clothes.' She couldn't understand it. 'Why would she bury all his things?'

'Yeah.' Kelly nodded grimly. 'My guess is that there's another plot around here, measuring six by three. And your Granddad's probably in it.'

'Cut it out, Kelly,' Charlene snapped.

Jane was shaking her head in disbelief. 'Nan wouldn't do anything like that,' she said in a voice that was barely audible.

'What are you doing?' a new and penetrating voice demanded.

They jumped in fright; they had been so intent on what had been buried in Mrs Mangel's garden that they hadn't been aware of Mrs Mangel herself bearing down on them with a look of fury in her eyes.

'Nan!' Jane exclaimed.

Wrapped loosely in her dressing gown, her hair dishevelled and a wild look in her eye, Mrs Mangel glared at them. 'Just what are you three up to?'

'Nothing, Mrs Mangel.' Charlene was standing in front of the disturbed earth while Kelly was trying to hide the clock behind her back.

'What have you got there?' Mrs Mangel advanced threateningly on Kelly.

'It's nothing, Mrs Mangel,' Charlene said nervously.

Mrs Mangel didn't take her eyes off Kelly. 'You give me what you've got there.'

'I haven't got anything,' Kelly muttered defiantly.

Mrs Mangel held out her hand. 'Don't lie to me, you nasty little thief.' Reluctantly, realising she had little choice, Kelly handed over the clock. 'It's stealing,' Mrs Mangel said severely as she clutched the clock to her. She frowned at Jane. 'Why did you allow these . . . these criminals into my back yard?'

Jane tried to soothe her. 'It's all right, Nan.'

'It's not all right, Jane,' the old woman snapped at her. 'I come out here and find you poking around in business that doesn't concern you. Now . . .' she stared ferociously at Kelly and Charlene. 'Get off my property! At once. Go on, get off! I'll call the police if you don't. They'll deal with you.'

'You'd better go,' Jane murmured to Charlene who was looking at her with an inquiring expression. 'Come on, Nan,' she said gently to her grandmother. 'We'd better go inside.'

Still holding the clock protectively against her, Mrs Mangel allowed Jane to lead her back to the house.

'How dare you allow those two hooligans on my property,' she said angrily when they were inside. 'Digging up my garden, interfering in my business. I've got a good mind to call the police.'

'I was worried about you, Nan,' Jane said quietly. 'Last night, when you were digging in the garden, you were burying that clock, weren't you?'

'And if I was?' Mrs Mangel said stonily. 'I'm perfectly entitled to bury anything I choose in my own garden.'

'But why? Why all those other things of Granddad's?'

'They're old things.' Mrs Mangel was suddenly vague again. 'Things he doesn't need.'

'But, Nan . . .' This wasn't making sense at all. 'That clock was a wedding present from Granddad. You always said how much you loved it.' Mrs Mangel's expression revealed nothing; she remained silent. 'Where is he, Nan?'

'I told you.' Mrs Mangel sighed deeply. 'He's gone.'

'But he's coming back, isn't he?'

'No.' Mrs Mangel rallied. She fixed Jane with a piercing look. 'He's never coming back.'

'But you've had arguments before,' Jane said incredulously. 'Once he's had time to calm down—'

'It's not a matter of calming down,' Mrs Mangel

said with fierce determination. 'He's gone, and that's it. He's gone away – and I never want to hear his name mentioned in this house again.'

Jane stared at her helplessly; she didn't know what to think.

Eleven

'You don't need anyone, Paul.'

'Look, Susan, you've got to appreciate my feelings. When you've had a relationship as totally destructive as mine was, it's not surprising that I should be wary of getting into another one.'

'Stop using your marriage to Terry as an excuse. You're not the first person to be disillusioned.'

'Yeah.' Paul smiled ruefully. 'Maybe you bounce back better than I do.'

Maybe she did; maybe she *was* more resilient. 'I think it's time I went home.' Going home to Clive at the end of each day made working for Paul Robinson bearable.

'Hang on, Susan,' Paul said as she picked up her bag from the desk. 'We're not just talking about work here.'

'I don't know what you're talking about.' Susan was losing patience with him; they had been over this before, many times. 'I happen to be marrying Clive. Do you think I'd throw that away on the offchance that you might wake up to yourself?'

'Susan . . .'

Abruptly, before she knew what he was doing, he had pulled her to him. She tensed momentarily, then, as his lips found hers, relaxed in his arms. Suddenly realising what was happening, she angrily pushed herself away from him. 'Oh, what am I doing?' she cried in self-disgust. 'I should have my head read.'

'Why?' Paul was regarding her shrewdly. 'You don't love Clive.'

'And you don't love *me*,' she retorted. 'It's just that you can't stand to see anyone else win – can you?'

'That's not true, Susan,' Paul protested. 'But if you marry Clive, you could ruin all our lives. Surely you must realise that.'

Susan was incredulous; he was being so totally selfish. 'I'm trying to *make* a life. For Sam and me. Clive loves us, which is more than you can say.'

'I could love you, too,' Paul said earnestly. 'If you'd give me the chance. Look,' he went on when Susan gave him a doubtful look. 'I'm just beginning to learn to live with myself again.' His eyes stared sombrely into hers. 'You don't know how difficult it is after all this time to admit to people that you really *do* need them.'

There was no doubt that he was speaking from the heart; Susan's attitude towards him softened a little. 'But we all do,' she murmured.

'Then just give me some time,' he pleaded. 'Just let me work it out. I promise I won't hurt you again.'

'I don't have any time. I'm getting married.'

'But you *can't* go through with it.' He sounded desperate; his eyes implored her.

'But I have to.' There was a catch in her voice. 'If it wasn't for Clive, I don't know what would have happened to Sam and me.'

'But you can't marry someone just because you're grateful,' Paul pointed out to her. 'Just because he's prepared to look after you and the baby. You marry because you love that person.'

Yes . . . Susan knew that only too well. And there was no doubt in her own mind that Clive did love *her*. 'What am I supposed to say to him? "Sorry, Clive, you've done nothing to deserve this, but it's all off"?'

Paul nodded solemnly. 'Something like that,' he said.

Now, looking at Paul and coming to terms with her feelings for him, Susan knew what her decision would be.

Because she and Clive were quite close, Susan sought out Daphne Clarke in her coffee shop for her advice. 'Would Clive come to you if he was unhappy?' she asked, after Daphne had taken her into the kitchen where they would have more privacy.

'I hope so.' Daphne was looking at Susan closely. 'But *is* something likely to make him unhappy?'

Susan sighed; she wasn't feeling good about this at all. 'No matter what I do, Clive will be hurt,' she said miserably.

'Has this anything to do with Paul?' Daphne asked shrewdly.

Susan nodded. 'He told me I wouldn't marry Clive.'

Daphne frowned in annoyance. 'He shouldn't have done that.'

'But it's true. I don't love Clive – not in the way I love Paul.'

'Then what are you going to do about it?'

The more she thought about it, the more obvious the answer became. 'Tell Clive the truth, I suppose,' she said distantly. 'It wouldn't be fair to marry him now.'

'It would only make it worse,' Daphne agreed.

'And I can't do that to Clive.' She took Daphne's arm. 'Try and look after him, won't you,' she implored intensely.

Daphne smiled briefly. 'I'll be there when he needs me.'

'Thanks, Daphne. You're a good friend.'

It wasn't easy telling Clive of her decision, breaking into his account of a woman who had brought her son along the surgery that afternoon in the belief that he had swallowed all her birth control pills. Clive's face fell; he looked stricken. 'But I thought it was agreed—'

'I'm sorry, Clive. I can't help it. I've changed my mind.' She could see how crushed he was by her decision. She tried to make it a little easier for him. 'You've been the best friend we've ever had, Clive.' There was a tremor in her voice; she was close to tears. 'All the things you've done for Sam and me . . .'

'But . . .' Clive was shaking his head uncomprehendingly. 'All I wanted was for it to be perfect. A home . . . you . . . Sam . . . maybe more kids later on.' His eyes were glistening; Susan could see the pain in them. 'I love you, Susan.'

'I know, and your love is something I will value dearly.' The tears welled up in her own eyes. 'But I can't return it, not in the way you'd like.'

Clive's eyes narrowed in suspicion. 'This hasn't anything to do with Paul, has it?'

It had everything to do with Paul. 'He cares for me,' Susan said softly. 'He wants us to build a future together.'

'And you believe him?' Now there was bitterness in Clive's voice. 'My God, Susan, haven't you been hurt enough? Do you *have* to lay yourself out like some damned carpet for him to walk all over?'

Susan was sure it wouldn't be like that. 'He promised he would never hurt me again.'

'Paul Robinson has hurt everyone who has ever loved him. He's the original kiss of death.' He gestured angrily. But he was fighting a losing battle and Susan hated herself for causing him so much pain.

'What has he done? Promised you marriage and a mansion on a hill?'

'We haven't talked about marriage yet,' Susan replied with some hesitation.

'Of course not,' Clive cried. 'And you never will. It will always be business first and you a sad last. And what about Sam? What about the kid, eh? Where does *he* fit into Paul's plans? Somewhere between the latest merger and a client's dinner party? No . . .' His voice was raised; his face was reddening. 'I'm not going to let this happen. You may not love me, but I'm not going to let you do this to yourself – or Sam. You have to use your head, Susan.'

'I *have* been using my head,' Susan said brokenly. 'And I was wrong. It's my heart I have to follow, not my head.'

Clive took her by the shoulders; he was shaking her, trying to make her see sense. 'Can't you see what you're doing?' he demanded forcefuly. 'You're throwing it all away – and you'll never find *anyone* who loves you as much as I do.'

Susan turned away from him, no longer sure if she was doing the right thing or not.

She had another talk with Daphne Clarke, this time in Daphne's house; she thought this would help her to get things clear in her own mind. She desperately needed to talk to someone about it. Paul and Clive; Clive and Paul . . . 'Clive's the warmest, kindest, most wonderful man in the whole world,' she said dejectedly as Daphne handed her a cup of the coffee she had just prepared. 'And Paul's entirely different. It's fireworks and misery, and I never know what will happen next.' She looked bleakly across the table at Daphne. 'I'm scared, Daph. I think I've just screwed up the best thing I've ever had.'

'Don't get carried away,' Daphne gently rebuked

her. 'I know it's going to be tough on all of you, but you'll get through it.'

Somehow, and eventually. Sure, it would be a matter of time. . . 'I just don't want to hurt Clive. He doesn't deserve it.' She sighed. 'He says that Paul won't marry me.'

'What do you think?'

'I don't know. He says he needs time to sort himself out. I don't know what that means.'

'I've known Paul for quite a while,' Daphne said gently. 'He's messed up, sure, but he's not a liar. I think he deserves a chance.'

Susan looked at her. 'Are you saying I should leave Clive?'

'All I'm saying is that you need to know what Paul thinks before you can decide that,' Daphne said. 'And the only way you can find that out is to ask him.'

Paul was still working back at the office. He looked up as she entered. 'I didn't expect you back tonight,' he remarked. 'How did he take it?'

Susan was nervous, but she was still determined to get some answers from him. 'Telling him was one of the cruellest things I've ever done,' she said, slumping down on the chair in front of his desk. 'And in spite of everything he still wants to marry me.'

'But you won't, will you?'

She regarded him steadily for a moment. 'Do *you* want to marry me, Paul?'

Paul looked momentarily startled; he shuffled some papers on his desk. 'I suppose . . . some day,' he muttered evasively.

'And what does some day mean to you?' Susan's suspicions had been confirmed; he was definitely not committing himself. 'Three months from now? Before Sam starts school? When?'

Paul was becoming flustered; he shuffled some more

papers. 'I hadn't thought that far in the future,' he said awkwardly. 'I just thought we'd get to know each other. Spend some time together. See how things work out.'

Susan was becoming angry with him; this was not what she wanted to hear at all. 'What are we talking about here?' she demanded to know. 'A business merger, or the lives of three people?' She was on her feet now, leaning over the desk from behind which he was looking uncomfortably up at her. 'Just answer me one question. Do you love me or not?'

He still wasn't prepared to commit himself. 'Well . . . love is a fairly potent word,' he said, looking away from her. 'I mean, of course I care about you very much—'

'You're even scared of saying it, aren't you?' Susan challenged him.

Paul frowned in irritation at being put on the spot like this. 'What do the words mean, anyway,' he muttered. 'I've heard them all before.'

'For God's sake, Paul,' Susan cried. 'Can't you let go of the past long enough to make a future?'

'I don't know,' Paul said wearily. 'I just can't go through all that again.'

'It's always *you*, isn't it?' Susan accused him. 'You don't have any idea what you're putting *me* through. You don't want me, and you're going to make damned sure no one else can have me, either.' That was it – that was it in a nutshell.

Paul tried to deny it, but Susan furiously brushed this aside. 'I can't go back to Clive. He deserves more than I can give him.' She stared down at Paul. 'So now what?'

'You've got a good job.' He gestured around the office. 'You've got a son, you've got a bright future. We'll be together.'

'No, we won't.' Susan had made up her mind once and for all. 'I'm right back where I started. Alone.' She turned to the door. 'So good luck, Paul,' she said, just before she closed the door behind her. 'I hope you find whatever it is you're looking for.'

Yes, alone . . . Her and Sam. They would move on somewhere else; they would start again; they had each other. She would go back to Clive's place now. She would write him a note if he wasn't there, and she was sure she would cry a little as she wrote it.